3/19

Soof

All rights reserved. Published by Scholastic Press, an imprint of Scholastic Inc., *Publishers since 1920*. SCHOLASTIC, SCHOLASTIC PRESS, and associated logos are trademarks and/or registered trademarks of Scholastic Inc.

The publisher does not have any control over and does not assume any responsibility for author or third-party websites or their content.

This book is a work of fiction. Names, characters, places, and incidents are either the product of the author's imagination or are used fictitiously, and any resemblance to actual persons, living or dead, business establishments, events, or locales is entirely coincidental.

Library of Congress Cataloging-in-Publication Data available

ISBN 978-0-545-84665-3

10 9 8 7 6 5 4 3 2 1   18 19 20 21 22

Printed in the U.S.A.   23

First edition, October 2018

Book design by Nina Goffi

SARAH WEEKS

Soof

Scholastic Press / New York

For the midwestern boy who gave me
the idea for this book.
This one's for you.

SW

CHAPTER ONE

More than a bird loves to sing

I saw a white rabbit with one bent ear hopping over a giant spoon filled with whipped cream. That's what it looked like to me anyway. I'd been lying on my back in the bed of my father's rusty old pickup truck all morning, watching clouds. I tapped the end of my nose once, twice, three times with my finger and wished I'd remembered to put on sunscreen.

"Aurora!" my mother called from the house. "Lunch!"

"Coming!" I called back, but I didn't move. I was busy watching the rabbit turn into a girl with a puffy white bow in her hair. Lindsey Toffle, a girl who sat in front of me at school, wore a bow like that sometimes. It was so big I had to lean over to one side in order to see the blackboard.

The cloud broke apart and drifted away, but I was still lying there thinking about Lindsey Toffle. She was the most popular girl in my class, and she didn't like me at all. It might have had something to do with the fact that I bit her once when we were in kindergarten, but (A) that was a long time ago, and (B) it hardly even left a mark. The main reason Lindsey Toffle didn't like me was because I was weird.

Sometimes, just for fun, when I walked down the hall I would hop on one foot or flap my arms and pretend to be a bird. Other times, also for fun, I would speak in a British accent or a language I'd made up called Beepish. I wore my T-shirts inside out because the tags bothered me even after my mother cut them out. I liked counting stuff, I was obsessed with coloring in the middle of *o*'s, and I had an annoying habit of dividing my sentences into two parts, with an (A) and a (B).

"Aurora!" my mother called again.

"Coming!"

I climbed out of the back of the truck and dusted myself off. Duck was busy digging a hole in the corner of the yard, shooting dirt out from between his hind legs like a maniac. When I whistled through my teeth, he stopped digging and came running. Duck was the sweetest, smartest, most loyal dog in the world, and as if that wasn't reason enough to love him, the inside of his ears smelled like popcorn.

I pulled open the screen door. "After you, guv'nor," I said in my best Cockney accent. Duck followed me into the kitchen and flopped down expectantly on the floor beside my chair.

"Don't think I haven't noticed you two are in cahoots," my mother said, setting a bowl of tomato soup and half a grilled cheese sandwich in front of me. "If I had a nickel for every scrap of food you've 'accidentally' dropped on the floor for that dog, I'd be a wealthy woman."

My father says the reason my mother's name is Ruby is because her parents took one look at her and knew she was a gem. She likes it when he says that. I can tell because her eyes sparkle.

"How's the quilt coming along?" I asked, biting off a corner of my sandwich. I had a system—corners first, then a row of tiny, evenly spaced bites across the top edge to make it look like waves. I counted sixteen bites in all, including the corners.

The quilt was for Heidi, a girl who had stayed with my parents for a little while before I was born. She wasn't a girl anymore; she was all grown up now and married to a very tall man named Paul. The quilt was for the baby Heidi was expecting, a little girl due in July.

"I'm almost finished with the border," my mother told me. "I don't know if Heidi will recognize the fabric, but it's from the curtains that used to hang in that back bedroom before it was yours. That's where Heidi slept when she was here."

"I know," I said, tapping the edge of the table once, twice, three times. Tapping was another weird thing I liked to do—always in threes, because three was my favorite number.

I'd never met Heidi, but I'd heard a lot of stories about her. There was the one about the jar of jelly beans and the one about the penny getting stuck in the vacuum cleaner. There was the one about Heidi's mama learning how to use the electric can opener and the one about Bernadette, Heidi's neighbor, making a bet with my father that Heidi could guess ten coin flips in a row without missing. I'd heard the Heidi stories so many times I knew them all by heart, but my favorite by far was the one about me. My mother always told it the same way:

"We'd been waiting for a baby of our own for a very long time. We'd all but given up hope. Then one day, out of the blue, a stranger arrived in Liberty. Her name was Heidi It. From the outside she looked like an ordinary girl, but inside she had a powerful streak of luck running through her like a river. Heidi didn't stay for very long, but her visit changed our lives forever. Before she left she passed her good luck along to your father and me, and the following winter, on a snowy Monday morning, you were born."

That was it. The whole story. But the message came through loud and clear: My parents had been given a whole lot of luck, and they'd used it all up wishing for me.

Duck whined to let me know he was tired of waiting.

"Beep-boop-beep-boop-bing-bing," I said.

"Translation, please," my mother replied. She was used to me speaking to her in Beepish.

"May I have some milk, please?" I asked.

My mother opened the fridge and grabbed the carton of milk. While her back was turned, I took the opportunity to drop a ribbon of crust on the floor for Duck, who quickly gobbled it down.

"It's hard to believe that Heidi's old enough to be having a baby," my mother said wistfully as she opened the cupboard and took out a tall glass with a cheerful ring of daisies painted around it. "It seems like only yesterday she was sitting at this very table eating blueberry pancakes."

"They weren't blueberry pancakes," I corrected. "They were regular pancakes with blueberry syrup."

"That's right," she said. "They were."

"That was the day Heidi was mad at Dad for going up

to Hilltop Home without her. Later he came back and got her, and that's when she met her grandfather for the first time."

My mother nodded and set the glass down in front of me, along with a multivitamin. She was wearing the yellow apron I'd given her for Mother's Day the year before.

"I worry you're not getting enough vitamin D," she told me. "It's important for your bones."

"Don't worry, Mom," I said, tapping the shiny orange tablet three times with my finger. "My bones are fine."

"Mothers are supposed to worry," she explained as she poured another inch of milk into my glass.

"That's not what Dad says. He says worrying is like a rocking chair. It's something to do to pass the time, but it doesn't get you anywhere."

My mother sighed. She was tired of people telling her not to worry, especially my father.

"Do me a favor and take your vitamin, will you, please?" she said.

As she took off her apron and hung it on a hook in the broom closet, I popped the vitamin in my mouth and took three quick sips of milk to wash it down. Thinking about Heidi eating those pancakes had gotten me thinking about Heidi's grandfather, who used to run the place where my mother worked before I was born.

"Thurman Hill's eyes were the same shade of blue as the chunk of sea glass Bernadette kept in her jewelry box," I recited matter-of-factly.

My mother turned and stared at me.

"What?" I said. "That's what Heidi said the first time she saw him, isn't it?"

"Word for word. But how is it that you can remember an obscure little detail like that, yet forget to put on sunscreen before you go outside?"

"Sorry, Mom," I said and began to nibble a new set of waves along the edge of my sandwich.

"I'll pick up some aloe lotion this afternoon at the drugstore," my mother told me.

"Could you tell by looking at Heidi that she had a lucky streak?" I asked when I'd reached the end of the row. Fourteen bites this time, because the corners were already gone.

"No," my mother answered. "But it's a good thing she did, because otherwise we wouldn't have you."

My mother always did that—connected Heidi's story with mine. Most of the time I didn't mind. But sometimes I wondered what it would feel like to have a story all my own, instead of having to share it with some girl I'd never even met.

I was swallowing the last spoonful of soup when my father strolled into the kitchen carrying a plastic bag full of frozen minnows. He was still wearing his uniform, but he'd left his hat in the car.

"You'd better not be planning to put those fish in my freezer, Roy Franklin," my mother warned.

"They're double bagged, Rube," he said, kissing her on the cheek. "Trust me, they hardly stink at all. Besides, it's just 'til tomorrow morning. Rory and I are going out on the lake first thing—right, baby girl?"

My father was the sheriff of Liberty. He was tall and handsome, with a thick brown mustache that sometimes made it hard to tell if he was being serious or pulling your leg. While he was on duty he carried a gun in a holster and a pair of handcuffs clipped to his belt. He wore a big gray hat and a gold badge, and when he walked into a room or drove down the street in his black-and-white cruiser, you could tell strangers were a little afraid of him. Anybody who really knew him, though, understood that hidden underneath that shiny gold star lay a heart as soft and warm as the dinner rolls at the Liberty Diner.

"Can Duck come too?" I asked.

At the mention of his name, Duck's tail thumped against the leg of my chair a couple of times.

"No way. He'll scare the fish away," my father complained as he opened the freezer door and tossed the bag of minnows in.

"Roy!" my mother scolded, playfully snapping the dish towel at him. "What did I tell you about those fish?"

He grinned and dodged the snapping towel.

"Trust me, Rube, it's the lesser of two evils," he said as he danced away from her. "The only thing more smelly than a frozen minnow is a thawed one."

She laughed and snapped the towel at him again.

"Save me, Rory!" my father cried, jumping behind my chair in mock terror.

"Only if Duck can come fishing with us tomorrow," I said. "Right, boy?"

Duck threw back his head and howled in agreement.

My mother flicked the towel once more. This time, instead of dodging it, my father reached out, caught hold of the end, and pulled her toward him.

"Family hug!" he shouted, and I jumped out of my chair to join them. We wrapped our arms around each other, and Duck howled again, which made everyone laugh.

When I think back on that moment now, all of us together in the kitchen, there's a golden glow around the memory, like a frame around a picture. It was nothing out of the ordinary. We were a close-knit family, but something was about to happen that would unravel my world, and it all started with Lindsey Toffle's silver charm bracelet.

CHAPTER TWO

More than a fish loves to swim

"Did you see this, Rube?" my father asked the next morning, pointing to an article on the front page of the Sunday paper. "They're tearing down Hilltop Home."

"What a shame," my mother said, looking over his shoulder at the picture. "It was such a beautiful place back in the day."

My father groaned.

"It says here they're putting in another Dollar General Store. Just what we need, huh?"

"More coffee, Roy?" my mother asked. "I can brew another pot."

I'd been up and dressed for hours.

"I thought you said we were going fishing first thing, Dad," I grumbled. "It's almost eight o'clock already!"

My father folded the newspaper and pushed back his chair.

"You grab the minnows, baby girl, and I'll get the poles," he said.

I helped him load the tackle box, net, and other gear into the back of the truck, and in record time we were rolling down the driveway, my mother calling after us, "Have fun, you two!"

"You mean us *three*!" I called back, pointing to Duck as I waved to her out the open window.

Twenty minutes later we were sitting in a rowboat, watching our red-and-white bobbers drift on the sparkling green surface of Bartlett Lake. Duck kept a lookout from the bow, snapping at passing horseflies.

"Your mother mentioned that she drove by the Toffles' house last night," my father said as he clicked open the lock on his reel and let out a little more line. "She said it looked like they were having some kind of a party."

"Yesterday was Lindsey's birthday," I explained.

"I kind of figured as much. How come you weren't invited?"

"I was," I told him. "I didn't feel like going."

I'd been excited at first when I'd found the pink envelope lying on my desk. I'd never been invited to one of Lindsey's parties before. This time the whole class was coming, even the boys. I'd heard there was going to be a DJ and a chocolate fountain for dipping strawberries— I'd seen one advertised on TV and was really looking forward to trying it out. Then during PE I overheard Lindsey telling one of her friends that the only reason she'd invited me was because her mother had told her she had to. When we got back to our classroom, I tore the invitation in half and threw it away. Even the promise of chocolate-covered strawberries wasn't enough to make me go someplace I knew I wasn't wanted.

My father got a nibble, but when he reeled in the line there was nothing but a tangle of slimy green weeds on the hook.

"Looks like we'll be having salad for dinner tonight," he said.

I laughed.

"Even if we catch a fish we're not going to bring it home," I said. "Mom would have a fit. I think she's making meat loaf and mashed potatoes tonight."

"I know," said my father. "I was making a joke."

We were both quiet for a while, the water slapping softly against the sides of the boat. Then Dad cleared his throat, and I knew something was coming.

"How's school going?" he asked.

"Regular," I answered cautiously.

"Nothing new?"

"Danny Lebson was out sick this week, so now I'm the only one in class who has a perfect attendance record.

Mr. Taylor says if I keep it up he'll bake me a cherry pie on the last day of school."

"That's nice," said my father, but it was clear there was still something on his mind. "Did I ever tell you that when I was your age, I used to get teased about my teeth?"

"They look okay to me," I told him.

"Sure, they are now, but before I got braces there was a boy in my neighborhood named Stevie Pritchett who used to call me Graveyard Franklin."

"How come?"

"He said my teeth were so crooked, my mouth looked like a cemetery full of old tombstones, all leaning in different directions."

"That was mean," I said.

He nodded and looked over at me. "Kids can be pretty mean sometimes."

I sighed. Here it was. The something I'd felt coming.

"Are we about to have a Mom talk?" I asked.

"What's a Mom talk?"

"You know. The ones where she asks me if kids are picking on me at school because I'm weird, and I tell her no, they just ignore me, and she says, doesn't that hurt your feelings, and I say not really, but she doesn't believe me so she asks me again and I tell her that I'm used to it and then she looks really sad."

I could tell by the look on my father's face that he knew what I was talking about.

"Your mother and I are both concerned for your happiness," he said.

Oh, brother. I was used to my mother fussing over me, but now my father was getting in on the action too?

"Here's the deal, Dad," I told him. "You can't both be concerned because that's *too much*. Like when the snow piles up on the roof and you have to go up there and shovel it off. Mom gets to be the worrier because she can't help it. You have to be the normal one who doesn't freak out about everything."

"I'll try," he said. "Can I finish my story now?"

I shrugged and he went on.

"One day on my way home from school I saw Stevie Pritchett coming up the street in my direction. I could tell by the look on his face that he was gearing up to say something mean, but instead of turning around or crossing over to the other side of the street the way I usually did, I reached into my pocket and pulled out a package of Wrigley's."

"What's Wrigley's?" I asked.

"It's a kind of gum."

"Why's it called Wrigley's?"

"That's not the point," he said. "Anyway, there was one stick of gum left in the pack, so I held it out to Stevie and asked him if he wanted it. He looked kind of surprised, but he took the gum, thanked me, and walked away."

"Let me guess, Dad. Did you and Stevie Pritchett become best friends after that?"

"Maybe not best friends, but definitely friends," he said.

"Where is he now?" I asked.

"I'm not sure. His family moved away after we graduated high school, and after that we lost track of each other."

"Wouldn't it be funny if Stevie Pritchett grew up to be an orthodontist?" I said.

"Huh?" My father tilted his head to one side.

"On account of what he said about your teeth being crooked," I explained. "Get it?"

Before he could respond, I felt a hard tug and the tip of my pole bent down so far I thought it might break right off. I knew what to do. I pulled in my elbows and jerked the line up and to the side to set the hook.

"Atta girl, Rory!" my father shouted, reaching for the net. "Reel it in nice and slow now. Looks like you've got yourself a real whopper!"

That fish put up a pretty good fight, but I took my time, letting it tire itself out so it would be easier to land. When it got close enough that we could see it, my father leaned over the edge of the boat and scooped it up.

"*What is it?*" I asked, wrinkling my nose in disgust at the hideous brown thing flipping and flopping in the net.

"Bullhead," my father told me. "I'm guessing six, maybe seven pounds."

Duck was so excited he nearly tipped us over trying to get close enough to sniff the fish.

"What are those gross things sticking out of its face?" I asked.

"Whiskers," my father said. "They won't hurt you—it's the fins you have to watch out for. They're sharp as all get-out, especially the one right behind his head."

"How do you know it's a he, not a she?" I asked. "Because of the whiskers?"

"No, all bullheads have whiskers, but the males have bigger heads, and their bodies are more narrow."

Unfortunately, the bullhead had swallowed the hook, so my father had to use a pair of pliers to pull it out. I didn't know fish could talk, but this one objected loudly with an awful belching sound until the hook was finally free and my father could toss him back into the water. Duck was so worked up by then, I thought he might jump right in after it.

"Easy, boy," I said, taking hold of his collar and pulling him away from the edge of the boat. "Remember, you're not a puppy anymore."

We weren't exactly sure how old Duck was. He had to be at least nine, because I'd been three years old when we got him. It was a few days before Christmas, and as my father was getting ready to leave the police station, someone showed up with a stray they'd found wandering around out on Route 52. The dog didn't have a collar or tags, and since no one was answering the phone at the animal shelter in Rock Hill, my father decided he had no choice but to bring him home.

"Duck!" I'd announced, the minute I laid eyes on that dog.

My mother had stopped short.

"Did you hear that, Roy?" she'd cried. "She's trying to say *dog*! Can you say *dog*, Aurora? Can you say *dog*?"

"Duck!" I'd said again.

Most toddlers were already talking in full sentences by the time they were three, but I had been slower in learning how to do a lot of things, including talking.

"Duck, duck duck!" I'd exclaimed as my mother clapped her hands delightedly.

The name stuck, and when nobody showed up to claim him, Duck became an official member of the Franklin family. He wasn't allowed up on the furniture, so he slept on a rag rug in the kitchen. After my parents went to bed,

I would often sneak out of my room and keep him company. In the morning my mother would find us sound asleep, curled up on the rug together.

I had no idea what Duck did all day while I was in school, but he was always waiting for me by the door when I got home. I wished I could bring him with me to school. He would've loved the cafeteria. People dropped all kinds of stuff on the floor. Besides, he could have kept me company. Duck and I understood each other. He didn't worry about whether I had enough friends or bug me about putting on sunscreen, and I didn't get mad at him if he rolled in something stinky or almost tipped the boat over when we went fishing.

The ugly old bullhead was the only thing we caught that morning at Bartlett Lake, but I didn't care. I was happy just to be there with Duck and to get some alone time with my father. Most mornings he was gone before I got up, and I was often asleep by the time he got home at night. Talking to him was easy, and we loved to make each other laugh. When we were done fishing, we pulled the boat up onto the shore and tucked the oars inside, the way my mother always tucked the tips of the wings under to keep them from drying out when she roasted a turkey. My father threw the anchor—an old Maxwell House coffee can filled with cement—out onto the ground and tossed a faded blue tarp over the boat.

"It's not even," I said, pointing to a corner of the tarp that was hanging down a little farther on one side than the other.

"Good enough?" he asked, giving it a tug.

I nodded and tapped the end of my nose once, twice, three times.

"Dad, if I ask you a question, do you promise to give me a true answer?" I said as we loaded the stuff in the back of the truck. "Was it Mom's idea for you to tell me that story about Stevie Pritchett?"

My father hung his head.

"Maybe," he said sheepishly.

"I knew it!"

"She was worried that your feelings might be hurt if you found out you hadn't been invited to Lindsey's party."

"But I *was* invited," I told him.

"I know. And next time maybe you'll go. The easiest way to make a friend is to be a friend."

"Like with you and Stevie Pritchett?" I said.

"Like with me and Stevie Pritchett," he agreed.

"Let's do this again real soon, baby girl," my father said a few minutes later as we climbed back into the truck.

"Okay," I said. "And Duck too, right? You have to admit, he was a good boy. Weren't you, Duckie?"

I patted his smooth black head and he closed his eyes with pleasure. Anybody who tells you that a dog can't smile doesn't know what they're talking about.

On the ride home, we turned the radio up loud and sang along at the top of our lungs, making up silly words to the songs we didn't know. Duck lay on the seat between us, dozing peacefully.

I loved that dog so much it hurt sometimes. He was my best friend. I couldn't even imagine what life would be like without him by my side.

CHAPTER THREE

More than a bell loves to ring

On Monday morning, Lindsey Toffle waltzed into class wearing a silver charm bracelet her grandmother had given her for her birthday. It was from some fancy-schmancy jewelry store in New York City, and Lindsey couldn't stop bragging about how much it must have cost.

During silent reading she took the bracelet off and left it sitting on her desk while she went to use the bathroom. I couldn't resist, and picked it up. I wasn't planning to steal it—I only wanted to see the charms up close. There was a little seahorse, a wishbone, a cup and saucer, a heart with an arrow shot through it, a musical note, and a tiny silver bell, each one dangling like a dewdrop in a spider's web.

"Who said you could touch that?" cried Lindsey as soon as she returned, snatching the bracelet away from me. Before she put it back on, she touched each one of the little charms to be sure that none were missing.

Later during recess, I noticed something shiny lying on the ground. When I bent down for a closer look, I discovered it was the little silver bell. It must have come loose and fallen off the chain somehow. Ever since my father had told me the story about Stevie Pritchett, I'd found myself wondering what it might feel like to have a friend besides Duck. Someone I could talk to, who would actually talk back. Maybe the silver bell would be my stick of Wrigley's gum. Maybe when I returned the charm to Lindsey, she would realize I wasn't so bad after all and want to be my friend. Maybe we'd even be best friends by the time we started middle school in the fall. I was so excited I could hardly breathe.

According to my mother, I had always been different from other kids. When I was a baby, I was sensitive to loud sounds and would scream and cover my ears in the grocery store every time they made an announcement over the PA system. My mother bought me the smallest pair of soundproof headphones she could find, and I would wear them when we went shopping or whenever she needed to run the blender or the vacuum.

There were no other children my age in our neighborhood, so my mother would load up a bag with snacks and sand toys and drive me to a playground a few miles away. Being an only child, I wasn't used to being around other children, and I didn't like them very much. My mother watched me like a hawk. If I pushed some little girl who came too close to me in the sandbox, or growled at an older boy who was trying to rush me up the steps of the slide, she would rush over to intervene, explaining to anyone who would listen that I didn't mean any harm, I was sensitive about my personal space.

I wasn't good at sharing and would pitch a fit if anyone tried to touch my things, kicking and flailing my arms. Eventually people began to avoid us, pulling their children out of the sandbox or off the swings when they saw us coming. I was perfectly happy to play by myself, in fact I preferred it, but it was hard for my mother. She stopped taking me to the playground and bought a swing set and sandbox to put in our backyard instead.

When I turned five, my mother told my father she thought it would be best if I were homeschooled.

"After all, Heidi was homeschooled, and look how well she turned out," she argued.

I would have liked nothing better than to stay home with my mother and Duck all day, but my father put his foot down.

"She's never going to learn how to stand on her own two feet if you're always there to catch her before she falls," he told her.

I didn't cry when my mother dropped me off on the first day of kindergarten, but the phone calls home began almost immediately. Not only had I bitten Lindsey Toffle during circle time, I was throwing temper tantrums at the drop of a hat. I was also a runner.

Our house was a good ten miles from school, but that didn't stop me from trying to get home. When things didn't go my way, I would take off running and never look back. I wasn't fast enough to outrun a grown-up, but I certainly winded a few. The minute someone spotted me, the cry would go up, "Aurora running!" A few minutes later I'd be hauled back inside and marched down to the principal's office. I spent a lot of time in the principal's office that first year, and sitting on the time-out bench, and talking to Mrs. Strawgate, the school counselor. She was the one who recommended that I be tested.

"For what?" my father asked. "Rory's already reading chapter books and she's only five."

My mother reached over and squeezed his arm.

"It can't hurt, Roy," she said.

I was given an IQ test, along with a bunch of other tests, all of which I passed with flying colors.

"Looks to me like we've got a little genius on our hands, Rube," my father said proudly.

"She doesn't have a single friend," she told him.

By the end of that year I had stopped running and learned to control my temper, but the damage was already done. Liberty is a small town. There were only fifteen kids in my grade, one of whom I'd bitten. Their minds were already made up about me.

The following year at parent-teacher conferences, my first grade teacher, Mrs. Rattner, mentioned that I preferred to play by myself at recess and that she'd noticed I touched my nose a lot and sometimes talked to myself.

Later that evening my mother told my father she'd made an appointment for me with a psychologist she'd found in Middletown.

"You're not serious, are you, Rube?" my father asked. "She's just a kid."

When my mother reached over and squeezed his arm, he knew there was no point in arguing.

* * *

Dr. Harris's office smelled like a mix of salami and BO. We played Chutes and Ladders while he asked me a lot of questions.

"What's your favorite thing about school, Aurora?"

"Coming home," I answered.

"What's your second favorite thing about school?"

"The drinking fountain," I said.

"Why's that?" Dr. Harris asked.

"(A) The water is really cold, and (B) if people push the button too hard it squirts them in the face. In case you're wondering, my third favorite thing is Henrietta and my fourth is Gordon."

"Are Henrietta and Gordon in your class?" asked Dr. Harris.

I giggled. Henrietta was a bunny who lived in the principal's office, and Gordon was the custodian.

"He's got a long pole with a tennis ball on the end for getting scuff marks off the floor," I explained. "He let me try it once. His favorite food is pimento cheese and mine is waffles. What's yours?"

"Black olives," Dr. Harris answered and jotted something down in his notebook.

When we were finished, Dr. Harris invited my mother to join us in his office.

"How did it go?" she asked, perching on the edge of the couch, her hands fluttering in her lap like a couple of nervous little birds.

"Aurora is clearly very bright," Dr. Harris told my mother. "She's articulate and has a delightful sense of humor, but like many only children, I gather she's more comfortable around adults than children."

"Do you think you can help her?" my mother asked.

"Help me with what?" I objected. "I'm only six and I beat him at Chutes and Ladders twice!"

Dr. Harris laughed.

"Therapy can be a long and involved process, Mrs. Franklin," he told my mother. "Aurora definitely marches to her own drum, but she seems quite happy to me."

"I'd be happier if Duck was here," I said. "Except he might scooch his butt on your rug."

"Aurora's teacher feels she tends to isolate from her peers," my mother explained. "And she has a number of unusual habits."

"Yes, I noticed the tapping," said Dr. Harris. "Repetitive behaviors are a common response to stress."

I was getting bored with the conversation.

"Can I color in your *o*'s?" I asked, pointing to a pile of magazines sitting on the corner of Dr. Harris's desk.

He looked confused.

"My what?"

My mother opened her purse and took out a ballpoint pen.

"Would you mind?" she asked, reaching for a copy of *Psychology Today* sitting on the top of the pile. "It might help keep her occupied while we finish talking."

I lay down on the rug and got to work filling in the three glossy *o*'s on the cover, while my mother finally mustered up the courage to ask a question that had been keeping her awake at night.

"I used to work at a place in Liberty called Hilltop Home. Maybe you've heard of it?" she began. "We saw a lot of autism and Asperger's, so I'm familiar with the signs. I've often wondered—I mean, as we discussed on the phone, Aurora had significant developmental delays, and she exhibits other telltale behaviors. Do you think it's possible she might be . . ."

"On the spectrum?" Dr. Harris said. "No, I don't."

"How can you be sure?" my mother asked. Her voice sounded shaky, as if she might be about to cry.

"Her interaction with me was completely appropriate, Mrs. Franklin. She was engaged, made eye contact, had inflection in her voice."

"If it's not ASD, then what is it?" my mother said. "OCD? ADD? It has to be *something*."

I looked up from my coloring.

"Are you mad, Mom?" I asked. "Because you sound mad."

"No, sweetie, I'm not mad. Just frustrated." She turned back to Dr. Harris. "I want the very best for my daughter. Early intervention is key. You realize that without a diagnosis, she'll get no services whatsoever."

"People are in such a hurry these days to pin a label on anyone who doesn't quite fit the mold," he responded. "Not everything has a name."

"I do," I said, putting the finishing touches on a nice round *o* I'd found in an advertisement for some pills. "Aurora."

My mother took me to see two more psychologists, plus an occupational therapist, all of whom came to the same conclusion: I was quirky, but not on the spectrum. I was also getting *very* good at playing Chutes and Ladders.

"Enough is enough," my father said when he saw the bills. "No more testing, no more shrinks. She is who she is, Rube. Let it be."

I had always been the center of my mother's attention. We were extremely close. She loved me with all her heart, and I was anxious to please her, even if it meant trying to make friends with someone who'd made it clear from the minute we met that she didn't like me. The reason I had

bitten Lindsey Toffle way back when we were in kindergarten was because she'd told me I couldn't sit next to her
on the rug because I was ugly. Now, I was filled with hope
as I hurried across the playground, clutching Lindsey's
silver charm tightly in my hand.

Lindsey and her friends were playing foursquare with
a rubber ball in a chalked box, slicing the air with their
palms to make the ball spin. If my plan worked, I could
be bouncing that very same ball back and forth soon
myself.

"What do you want?" Lindsey asked when she noticed
me standing there watching her.

Suddenly I felt nervous.

"I just wanted to . . . I thought m-maybe you . . . ," I
stammered.

"Maybe I what?" Lindsey asked, slapping the ball so
hard it bounced outside the line. "No fair! I get a do-over.
Aurora was distracting me."

"Lindsey?" I said, stepping forward.

"What do you want?" she snapped, spinning around
on her heel to face me. "Can't you see I'm busy?"

"I thought you'd like to know—I mean, I wanted to tell you that—"

"Tell me what? That you're a freak?" she said.

Then she crossed her eyes and tapped her nose with her finger three times.

The nasty look on her face reminded me of that ugly old bullhead. Only the whiskers were missing.

Lindsey's friends had stopped playing and were watching us now, whispering to each other behind their hands and laughing. A small crowd began to gather. Like most bullies, Lindsey Toffle loved an audience.

"Hey, Aurora Franklin!" she shouted at me. "Why don't you show the whole world your flowered undies again?"

I knew I should walk away, but I couldn't move. It was as if my feet had grown roots. I wanted to tell Lindsey that (A) thanks to her, I didn't wear flowered underwear anymore, and (B) I hadn't meant for anyone to see them. We'd been in second grade when it happened. I'd been fooling around on the monkey bars by myself during recess one day. After hooking my knees over one of the bars I'd let go with my hands, forgetting that I had on a dress. The next thing I knew, my dress was around my ears and Lindsey Toffle was laughing her head off, telling everyone to come look at my underwear.

Later that day when I got home from school, I'd told my mother I needed some new underwear.

"I bought you three pairs last week," she'd said. "Yellow with pink roses. They're in your top drawer, sweetie."

"From now on I only want white," I'd told her, and hurried off to my room before she could ask me why.

"Earth to Aurora. Do you have something to say to me or not?" Lindsey asked now, her eyes gleaming the way Thurman Hill's sea-glass eyes must have looked the day Heidi showed up at Hilltop Home asking him a million questions he didn't want to answer.

I wanted to tell her that just because a person acts a little different, or accidentally showed their underwear on the playground once, doesn't mean they don't have feelings like everyone else. How would she feel if nobody ever wanted to play with her, or sit next to her at lunch, or had ever picked her, even once, to work with them on a school project? There were a lot of things I wanted to say, but the words got stuck in my throat, piling up until I felt as though I'd swallowed a mouthful of rocks.

"Well?" said Lindsey.

It was obvious this wasn't going to be my Wrigley's moment. Lindsey Toffle and I were not going to be friends. Ever.

"Never mind," I said, slipping the silver bell into my pocket and walking away.

CHAPTER FOUR

More than a wheel loves to spin

When we came back inside after recess, Lindsey was slumped down in her seat, crying. Mr. Taylor explained what had happened and asked the class if anyone had seen the missing charm. I folded my hands on top of my desk and didn't say a word. I had never kept a secret before, and I was surprised by the way it made me feel like a jar full of lightning bugs.

Later that afternoon when I got home, I went out to the garage and dug around in the recycling bin until I found an old metal Band-Aid box with a hinged top. After stuffing it full of cotton balls—eleven in all—I tucked the little silver bell inside and snapped the lid closed.

I considered several hiding places before settling on one. I figured that because I made my own bed every morning and changed the sheets myself every other Sunday, no one would ever have a reason to look under my mattress. Lifting up one corner, I slid the box under, carefully smoothing the covers when I was finished. I smiled to myself, enjoying the special sparkly feeling bubbling away inside me.

By morning, the special feeling was gone, replaced by a twisted-up pretzel of guilt. Keeping something that doesn't belong to you isn't the same thing as keeping a secret. It's stealing. Not only that, but I had lied to Mr. Taylor, my favorite teacher in the whole world. I could hardly wait to get to school. As soon as the coast was clear, I dropped the silver bell on the floor near Lindsey's desk where I was sure she would find it. As the knots in my stomach began to loosen, I crossed my heart and swore up and down that I would never, ever keep anything that didn't belong to me again.

It wasn't too long before I broke that promise.

A few weeks later during Easter vacation, my mother asked me to go check and see if the mail had been delivered yet. Duck came along, trotting down the driveway beside me with his tongue hanging out one side of his mouth. The little red flag on the side of the mailbox was up, and as I stepped out onto the road to pull open the flap, I kicked up something hard with the tip of my shoe. At first I thought it was a stone or a rusty bolt that had come loose and fallen off a passing car, but it turned out to be a cigarette lighter, the old-fashioned metal kind, like the one my uncle James used to light his pipe.

Duck gave it a quick sniff, but he was far more interested in the grasshoppers that were jumping around in the tall weeds. *Doggie Cheetos*, I called them, because they were one of Duck's favorite snacks when he was lucky enough to catch one.

Clearly the lighter had been there for a while. The outside was caked with dried mud. I turned it over and scraped the bottom with my fingernail the way my father scratched off the numbers on the Quickie Chance lottery tickets he bought at the gas station sometimes. As the dirt flaked away, letters appeared. *Z-I-P-P-O. Zippo.*

One time when my uncle James was visiting, I'd asked him to show me how his lighter worked. Uncle James lived in Sacramento and taught science in a private middle school for brainiac kids. We hardly ever got to see him. He looked exactly like my father, except that his hair was red instead of brown and his mustache was skinny. He put some kind of special wax on the ends to make them curl up. We were out in the backyard because my mother had told him he couldn't smoke in the house. He flipped open the lighter—*svvvit!* Inside was a little metal wheel that he had to push down with his thumb to make a spark to light the wick.

"Can I try?" I'd asked, reaching for the lighter.

My mother saw us from the kitchen window and came running.

"Have you lost your mind?" she'd yelled at Uncle James.

"I was only showing her how it worked, Ruby," he'd explained. "She was curious."

"In case you haven't heard, curiosity killed the cat," my mother had said, snatching the lighter away from him and storming back into the house.

"Wow," said Uncle James, shaking his head. "Your mom used to be so chill back in the day. Since when did she become such a worrywart?"

"Since forever," I'd told him.

Later that night, when my father had come into my room to say good night, I'd asked him why my mother worried so much.

"That's one of the ways she shows her love," he'd said.

"Like when Duck licks my face?" I'd asked.

He'd smiled and kissed my forehead.

"Yeah," he'd said. "Only without the slobber."

I wondered if the lighter I'd found in the grass worked the same way as Uncle James's had. I pried open the top with my fingers. Inside was the same type of notched wheel, only when I pushed down on it with my thumb, it didn't budge. I tried a few more times, but it was jammed tight. I didn't care if it was broken—I still thought it was cool. I wanted to keep it, but I knew there was no way on earth my parents would ever let me—especially not my mother. I wasn't even allowed to make popcorn in the microwave, for fear that I might burn my fingers opening the bag.

I turned the lighter over. It fit so perfectly in my palm, and I couldn't explain why, but there was something exciting about that word, *Zippo*. What if I didn't tell my parents about the lighter? After all, it didn't work, and there was no way I could return it to its rightful owner. It was probably some city person passing through, or someone who had chucked it out the window because it didn't work anymore. Why shouldn't I keep it if I wanted to? What harm could it do?

"Finders keepers, losers weepers," I whispered, closing my fingers around the lighter as that lightning-bug feeling came bubbling back up inside me. I had a real secret this time, one of my very own.

I skipped up the driveway and hopped up the porch steps backward just for the heck of it, tapping the railing three times before I went inside.

"Anything interesting today?" my mother asked as I handed her the mail.

"Blimey, yer ladyship, see fer yourself," I told her.

"Look!" she exclaimed happily, holding up a pale yellow envelope. "It's a letter from Heidi!"

It had been almost thirteen years since Heidi had traveled alone from Reno, Nevada, to Liberty, New York, on the wings of a mysterious four-letter word. After Heidi went home, she and my mother kept in touch, exchanging cards on major holidays and picture postcards if either of them went someplace interesting. At the bottom of each one they would always write the same thing: *soof*.

"What does it mean?" I'd asked my mother one day when I was a little girl.

She opened the flowery birthday card she'd bought for Heidi and uncapped her pen.

"*Soof* was Heidi's mama's special word for love," she explained.

"Why did she need a special word?" I asked, reaching for the pen as soon as my mother was finished writing so that I could color in the middle of those two beautiful little *o*'s.

"Because Heidi's mama was special," she said.

"Am I special?"

"Yes." She kissed the top of my head. "You are, but not in the same way."

When my mother had worked as an aide at Hilltop Home, one of the people she'd helped take care of was Heidi's father, Elliot. Heidi's mother had lived at Hilltop for a little while too, but that was before my mother's time, so they'd never actually met. I'd never met any of them, but I'd seen pictures.

Luckily my mother was too busy fussing now over the new letter from Heidi to notice the small lump in the back pocket of my jeans. I left her in the kitchen and went to my room. After closing the door, I took out the lighter and polished it with the hem of my T-shirt until it gleamed like a jewel. I didn't have the Band-Aid box anymore, so instead I put the lighter inside a pink sock that had lost its mate and tucked it under the mattress for safekeeping.

Over the next few days I took it out every chance I got, practicing flipping open the top until I could do it in a single motion, the way Uncle James did—*svvvit!* If my parents noticed that I was spending more time than usual alone in my room with the door closed, they didn't say anything about it. My father was busy at work, and my mother had other things on her mind, like washing the windows and polishing the silver. The reason Heidi had written was to say that she was coming to visit, and my mother wanted everything to be perfect.

"Don't let me forget to get the jelly bean jar down from the attic before Heidi gets here," she told me. "She'll want to see that again, I'm sure."

Heidi had won a free taxi ride by guessing the exact number of jelly beans in the jar when she'd first arrived in Liberty. There were 1,527 originally, but she'd eaten a few so now there were only 1,521. I knew that because I'd poured them out on the table and counted them one day when I was bored. There were 422 reds, 392 oranges, 275 greens, 220 yellows, 114 blacks, and 98 pinks.

While my mother was busy dusting and mopping and washing and waxing everything in sight, I was busy too, dripping oil onto the little wheel inside the lighter, trying to get it to move, but it was stuck as tight as ever. I even tried using coconut oil, but all that did was make it smell like a macaroon. After a while my excitement about the lighter began to wear off and the sparkly special feeling lost its fizz, like a bottle of soda gone flat. By the time school started up again, I had forgotten all about it.

CHAPTER FIVE

More than a spark loves to fly

My parents' thirtieth anniversary was May eighteenth. Dad had been up in the attic for weeks, working on a surprise for my mother. He was refinishing an antique steamer trunk that had belonged to her great-grandmother Alpha. First he'd taken off the tarnished brass hardware and soaked everything in vinegar, then he'd spent hours carefully sanding the dark oak panels, rubbing them with old T-shirts soaked in linseed oil to bring out the grain. He worked on the chest every chance he got, mostly on weekends, and it was my job to be his lookout.

If I saw my mother coming up the driveway from town or heading into the house after hanging up the wash, I would signal him by knocking on the ceiling in my room with the end of a wooden broom handle. A constellation of little black marks dotted the plaster above my bed from all that tapping.

Saturday morning, my mother spent several hours working on Heidi's baby quilt in the living room and listening to WJFF on the radio. I would check on her every fifteen minutes or so, then report back to my father, who was keeping busy out in the garage getting the recycling ready for a dump run until the coast was clear and he could go upstairs to his workshop.

After lunch, my mother finally put her sewing away and went off to the Stop & Shop to buy fixings for a special dinner she had planned. As soon as she was gone, I ran and got my father.

"Come take a look and tell me what you think," he said.

Duck followed me up the narrow stairs to the attic, where he made a beeline for the mouse hole he'd discovered the last time we'd been up there together.

"Think she'll like it?" my father asked as he picked up a dirty rag and tossed it onto a pile in the corner.

"I bet she cries when she sees it," I said.

The chest was beautiful. The brass hinges glistened like golden fish in the pool of warm sunlight that poured in through the skylights. Even with the windows open, it was hot up there.

I tapped my right elbow three times, then my left so they'd be even.

"You okay?" my father asked, glancing over at me.

I knew why he was asking. I tended to tap more when I was anxious.

"I'm fine," I told him, even though it wasn't true.

"You're not feeling nervous about Heidi's visit, are you?" he asked, wiping the sweat off his face with his sleeve.

My father knew me too well. All my mother had been able to talk about lately was Heidi's visit. She'd even planned the meals she was going to serve right down to the dessert. I knew all the Heidi stories backward and forward, but I didn't know her. I was worried she wouldn't like me. Or that my parents would decide they liked her better than me.

"Why should I be nervous?" I asked, resisting the urge to tap again and biting the inside of my cheek three times instead. "She's a nice person, right?"

"Very nice," my father said. "You'll be sharing your room with her. Are you going to be okay with that?"

"Does she snore?" I asked.

My father laughed.

"I guess we'll find out soon enough, won't we?" He took the cap off the bottle of linseed oil and poured some on a clean rag.

"Dad?" I said, unable to hold it inside any longer. "Does Heidi know that I'm weird?"

He stopped what he was doing and looked at me, his face all sad and soft.

"I wish you wouldn't say that, baby girl," he told me. "You're not weird, you're wonderful, and Heidi is very excited to meet you."

"How do you know?"

"She said so in her letter. Ask your mom if you don't believe me."

"What if Heidi doesn't like me?" I asked.

"What's not to like?" he said, screwing the cap back onto the bottle of oil and setting it aside. "Now scoot and let me finish up before your mom gets home, okay?"

Right before dinner, my father brought the chest downstairs and presented it to my mother. Just as I'd predicted, she burst into tears the minute she saw it.

"Oh, Roy! It's the most beautiful thing I've ever seen."

"I told you she was going to cry," I said.

"I'm afraid my gift pales in comparison to yours," my mother said, wiping away her happy tears. "I made you a pie."

"Lemon chess?" my father asked hopefully.

My mother nodded, and he let out a happy whoop.

"You know how I feel about your pie, Rube."

"She made real whipped cream to go with it too," I told him. "Not the fake stuff from a can."

"I guess mine wasn't the only secret you've been keeping, huh, baby girl?"

"It was my idea to put a fan in the window so you wouldn't smell the pie baking," I admitted.

"Come to think of it, how on earth did you manage to do all that work on Great-granny's chest upstairs without my even noticing, Roy?" my mother asked.

"Rory was my lookout," my father said proudly, throwing his arm around my shoulders. "She's a regular James Bond."

"James who?" I asked.

"Bond. James Bond. He's a famous spy," my father explained.

"Like Inspector Gadget?" I said.

My mother laughed. "Yes, only James Bond is very handsome."

"Hey," said my father. "What about me?"

"You're far more handsome than James Bond, and our daughter is an excellent double agent," my mother said. "I didn't suspect a thing."

"The chest isn't quite finished," my father explained. "The wood is old and thirsty. It's going to need a couple more coats of oil. I'll get on that right after dinner."

I ran my fingers over the smooth top.

"I sure wish I had something like this in my room. I could (A) keep summer clothes in it in the winter, and (B) keep winter clothes in it in the summer. That way I wouldn't ever run out of hangers."

"Oh, no you don't," my mother teased. "You may have your father wrapped around your little finger, but this chest belongs to me. Even if I have to spend the next thirty years baking pies to pay him back for it."

My father grinned and pulled her close.

"Happy anniversary, Rube," he said and leaned in to give her a kiss.

Duck barked and wagged his tail, the way he always did when anyone hugged or kissed each other in our house. It made me happy too.

We had steak and twice-baked potatoes for dinner. There was garlic bread with parsley butter, green beans, and of course, the lemon chess pie for dessert. There were even candles and fresh flowers on the table.

After the dishes were done, my father opened a bottle of champagne and some sparkling cider for me. We clinked glasses and made toasts to everyone we could think of, including the mailman, even though he wasn't particularly fond of Duck.

"What about Heidi's baby?" I said. "Shouldn't we toast to her?"

"Absolutely," said my father. "Do we know what they're planning to name her yet?"

It had been Heidi's idea to call me Aurora, on account of something Bernadette had once said about the importance of having a promising name.

"I haven't heard anything about a name yet," said my mother. "But if I had to guess, I expect she'll be called Sophia, after Heidi's mama."

"Maybe she'll be lucky, like Heidi was," I said.

"That would be nice," my mother agreed.

My father raised his glass.

"To baby Sophia," he said.

"And to luck," my mother added.

"And to Duck!" I said. "Because it rhymes!"

We clinked glasses, and after a few more toasts my parents were both a little tipsy and I was ready for bed.

After putting on my nightgown and brushing my teeth, I turned off the light and stared out the window at the moon for a while. I wondered why stars looked round up close and pointy from far away. I wondered how the same sky could look blue during the day and black at night. I wondered if Heidi was nervous about meeting me too, and whether she would remember what color the jelly beans were that she'd eaten before she gave the jar to my mother. Eventually, all that wondering made me sleepy, and I pulled the covers up to my chin and closed my eyes.

                        *   *   *

In the middle of the night, Duck started barking. Sometimes he did that when raccoons raided the bird feeders or a skunk wandered into the yard to rummage around in the compost heap, but this was different. He sounded scared.

"Rory!" my father shouted, bursting into my room. "Come quick! The house is on fire!"

I jumped out of bed and ran into the hall. Dark smoke was billowing down the attic stairs. Duck was frantic, running back and forth, barking his head off.

"Cover your mouth and nose with this," my mother said, handing me a damp washcloth. The light bulb in the fixture above our heads flickered and buzzed, then suddenly burst with a loud pop. I screamed, and my father scooped me up in his arms, like a fish in a net. I clung to him as he carried me through the house while my mother, in a robe and slippers, hurried along behind us, clutching her purse and her jewelry box.

Down the hill, the firehouse siren had already begun to blare, and soon the trucks arrived, carrying their bleary-eyed crews of volunteers.

I felt like I was a million miles away, watching the scene from outer space. This couldn't really be happening. Not to us. The air was thick with smoke, and it looked as if a fire-breathing dragon had crawled into the attic and was shooting bright orange flames through the roof. *Our roof.* One by one, the windows began to break.

"Everyone get out okay, Sheriff?" asked one of the firemen. It was Dave Toffle, Lindsey's father. I noticed he was still wearing pajamas under his rubber coat.

"Yes," my father told him. "We're all here."

But when I looked around, I realized he was wrong.

"Where's Duck?" I asked.

CHAPTER SIX

More than a mouse loves to nibble

When you turn a fire hose on full force and point it at the window of a burning house, as the water goes in, random things come flying out. Clothes, books, shoes, CDs lay scattered across our roof like seashells on a shingle beach. The first thing the firefighters had done was break through the skylights in the attic to draw the smoke and flames upward and away from the rest of the house. The yard quickly became a muddy mess; shards of glass and splintered wood lay everywhere. One of my mother's straw gardening hats ended up in the bushes somehow, along with a Popsicle stick reindeer ornament I'd made in kindergarten. The boxes of Christmas decorations were all stored up in the attic, along with our summer clothes and a lot of other things, but none of that mattered at the moment.

"We need to go back inside," I sobbed. "We have to find Duck."

The three of us were standing at the end of the driveway, watching the house burn.

"Fellas!" my father shouted to a couple of men hurrying by with pickaxes slung over their shoulders. "There might be a dog inside."

"His name is Duck!" I called after them. "He's black with a red collar."

They nodded and kept walking.

When my mother realized I was barefoot, she quickly gave me one of her slippers, and we each balanced on one foot like a pair of flamingos, watching the smoke turn from black to brown and finally to gray. One of the neighbors brought us a couple of blankets and a thermos of hot coffee. My mother handed one blanket to my father and wrapped the other around the two of us like a cocoon. She was shivering, but I was too worried about Duck to notice the cold.

When the fire was finally out and the firemen began to roll up their hoses, Dave Toffle came over to talk to my father. There was a dark streak of black soot across one of his cheeks, and his eyes were rimmed with red.

"Them skylights were a lucky break, Sheriff, 'cause we got in quicker than if we'd had to cut a hole. Pretty sure you're gonna need a new roof though. Chief's in there right now looking things over."

"What about Duck?" I asked anxiously.

"Duck?"

"My dog," I explained. "He's black with a red collar."

Dave Toffle shook his head.

"We didn't find any dog," he said. "Not as far as I know."

"Did you check in the kitchen?" I asked, tapping my

chin. "That's where he sleeps. Did you look in my room? He might be there too."

Lindsey's father wiped his cheek, adding another streak of soot to his face.

"Like I said before, we didn't find any dog." There was something not very nice about the way he said it that reminded me of Lindsey.

"What happens now?" my mother asked, looking forlornly at the house.

"Here comes Howie," my father told her. "He'll know."

Howard Strauss was the fire chief of Liberty. He and my father had played high school football together and had remained good friends.

"Sorry about the mess," he told us. "Other than the roof, though, you're pretty lucky. Most of what you'll have to deal with inside is smoke and water damage."

"Any idea what caused the fire?" my father asked.

"We know it started up in the attic, but as far as the cause goes, we're going to have to call this one undetermined," he said.

"Undetermined?" my mother asked. "Why?"

"It could have been any of a number of things," he said. "That bare bulb you had hanging up there might be the culprit. Or could be you had some rotting insulation. Even a mouse chewing through a wire could have caused a spark."

I thought about the mouse hole Duck had found.

"I do need to ask you about something though, Roy," he went on. "There's a good-sized burn mark in one corner. Any idea what might have caused that?"

My father's face fell.

"I'm sorry, Rube," he said, turning to my mother. "I took your chest upstairs last night after you went to bed, to give it another coat of oil. There was a pile of rags in the corner."

"Oily rags?" asked Chief Strauss. "That would explain the black smoke."

"I should have known better," my father said, shaking his head. "That was dumb."

My mother laid her head on his shoulder.

"It's okay, Roy. What matters is that we're all safe."

Had she forgotten about Duck?

"Can we go back inside now?" I asked. "To look for Duck?"

"I'm afraid I can't let you do that, Aurora," the chief said. "We did our best to find your pup though. The guys looked in every room."

"I can find him," I said. "I know I can."

Chief Strauss shook his head.

"We had to turn off the electric and gas at the junction box. There's no juice, so it's pitch-black in there. Not safe."

"We have flashlights in the garage," I said. "I'll go get one."

My mother put her hands on my shoulders to hold me back.

"How long before it will be safe to go inside, Howie?" she asked. "We're going to need some clothes, and Roy's heart medication."

I didn't know he took medicine for his heart.

"Are you sick, Dad?" I asked.

"It's nothing," he said. "Just a murmur. I've had it since I was a kid."

"I can come by and take a look around first thing in the morning?" Chief Strauss offered. "Daylight's only a few hours away. We'll get the roof wrapped up, and if the structure's sound, you folks can go inside long enough to get what you need. In the meantime, you'll have to find someplace to stay."

"I'm not leaving without Duck," I insisted.

"We can stay with Julie and Scott," my mother said, unwrapping the blanket and releasing me from the cocoon.

Julie Graham and my mother had been childhood friends. She and her husband, Scott, owned a garage in Youngsville.

"Darn. I left my phone inside," my father said, patting the nonexistent pockets of his pajamas.

"I've got mine," my mother told him, reaching for her purse and the jewelry box, which were sitting nearby on a rock. "I'll call Julie on the way."

"Wait," I said. "What about Duck? We can't just leave him here."

"We'll come back and look for him when it's light out," my father said to me. "Everyone knows to keep an eye out for him. With all the commotion going on around here he probably got scared and found himself a safe place to hide until the dust settled."

"I'll bet you anything he's waiting for us on the porch in the morning," my mother agreed.

"I'm not leaving without him," I insisted, but my parents were already heading up the driveway, my mother limping along in her single slipper. I stood for a moment in the moonlight, my nightgown fluttering like a circle of white moths around my knees, until I heard the car start up and my mother calling my name.

"Don't be afraid," I whispered into the cold night air. "I'll come find you, Duck. I promise."

CHAPTER SEVEN

More than a breeze loves to blow

"I gotta go to work now, hon," Julie whispered in my ear. I cracked open one eye and looked at the clock. It was seven thirty. "The twins are still asleep—they had a late game last night, and Scott's down at the garage. He doesn't usually work on Sundays, but it seems like everyone and their uncle needs an oil change all of a sudden.

Help yourself to anything in the kitchen if you're hungry. Mi casa es su casa."

I sat bolt upright.

"Where are my mom and dad?"

"They've gone over to the house already," she told me.

"To look for Duck?"

"They're meeting with the fire chief, but your father took a package of hot dogs along. I'm sure that pooch of yours will come running once he catches a whiff of those franks. He better—they're the expensive kind, all beef!"

As soon as Julie left, I called the house, but the electricity must not have been turned back on yet because the message machine didn't pick up. I tried both cell phones too, but they went straight to voicemail. My back ached, and I felt like a wrung-out dishrag. I hadn't slept well on the soggy blow-up mattress Julie had set up for me on the floor of her sewing room. I was worried sick about Duck.

Sometimes when I felt sad, I would crawl under our dining room table at home. It was old and made of dark wood, the curved legs ending in feet carved to look like lion's paws. After a while, Duck would come looking for me. If I was crying, he'd lick the tears off my face, and if I felt like being quiet, he knew to lie down beside me and be quiet too. I didn't have the dining room table right now, or Duck, so I pushed a basket of paper dress patterns out of the way and curled up under Julie's sewing table. A hunk of hair fell across my face. It smelled of smoke and so did my nightgown. Julie had offered me a pair of clean pajamas one of her boys had outgrown, but they had tags in both the top and bottom and I didn't have the energy left to explain why that would be a problem. Closing my eyes, I sent up a silent prayer that when my parents returned, Duck would be with them. I pictured him bounding through the door, jumping up on me to lick my face. I would press my nose into his popcorn-scented ears and tell him how sorry I was that I'd left him behind.

It was raining. Big round drops swam down the window-panes like fat tadpoles. It was a tighter squeeze under the sewing table than I was used to, and the big metal foot pedal dug into my back. When my legs began to cramp, I crawled out and headed to the kitchen for some breakfast. There were various kinds of cereal on top of the refrigerator. Without even thinking, I quickly reorganized them, turning the boxes so they all faced in the same direction and lining them up by height. After considering my options, I poured myself a bowl of Froot Loops and grabbed a spoon out of the drawer. There were a bunch of purple pens with *Youngsville Garage* written on them jammed into a chipped coffee mug beside the phone. I pulled one out and between bites colored in the four *o*'s on the front of the cereal box.

When I was finished, I carried my empty bowl over to the sink and noticed my mother's jewelry box sitting on the counter. When I was little I had loved to play dress-up with a pair of shiny gold bangles my father had given her, slipping them over my wrists, all the way up my skinny little arms. I rinsed out my cereal bowl and put it in the dishwasher, then I undid the clasp on the red leather box and lifted the lid.

There was a section in the middle where my mother kept her rings, each one pressed into a padded groove covered in velvet. I took a minute to organize those as well, grouping all the rings with stones together. On one side of that section were my mother's earrings, neatly hooked together in pairs, and on the other a jumble of beads coiled like colorful snakes. I started to reorganize those as well, until I remembered the reason I'd opened the box in the first place was to look for the gold bangles. Where could they be? I wondered. After digging through the beads I recalled that the box had another layer, a hidden compartment on the very bottom.

I lifted out the top section, and sure enough, there were my mother's bracelets—including the gold bangles. There was something else familiar: a pale yellow envelope. The first thing that occurred to me was that my mother had hidden the letter because what my father had told me wasn't true. Maybe Heidi wasn't looking forward to meeting me at all, and my mother didn't want me to find out because it might hurt my feelings. I thought about what my mother had said to Uncle James that day in our backyard. *Curiosity killed the cat.* Then I tapped the corner of the yellow envelope once, twice, three times and lifted the flap.

Heidi's letter was written on paper the same shade of yellow as the envelope. Her handwriting was small and neat, the letters slanting to the left like rows of little sailboats in a stiff breeze. I quickly skimmed the first page and halfway down the second found the part about me. My father had been telling the truth. Heidi had written that she was very much looking forward to meeting me in person.

I was certain that the visit was off now, because of the fire. My mother wouldn't dream of having company come with the house in the state that it was in.

Part of me was disappointed that Heidi wouldn't be coming, but most of me was relieved. I hadn't been looking forward to having to share my room with a stranger. Besides, with Duck missing I needed to focus all my attention on finding him.

As I was slipping the letter back into the envelope, I discovered that Heidi had sent my mother something else as well. A photograph. It was a faded picture of my mother standing in our front yard, her arms wrapped around a young girl with short brown hair.

Heidi.

I had never seen this picture before, but I knew the story well. The day after Heidi found out that her mama had died, she'd been so upset, she'd chopped off all her hair. I studied their faces carefully. Heidi was smiling at the camera, but you could tell that she'd been crying. My mother was smiling too, but there was something funny about her eyes. Something I couldn't quite put my finger on.

I heard the front door open.

"Rory?" my father called.

Quickly I jammed the photograph back in the envelope, tossed it in the jewelry box, and slammed the lid.

My father's wet hair was plastered to his forehead, and the legs of his jeans were dark from the knees down.

"Did you find Duck?" I asked, anxiously scanning the room.

My father shook his head.

"We called and called, but he never came. I left a

message at the animal shelter, so they'll know to keep an eye out for him."

"I need to go home," I said. "Right now. What if Duck comes back and there's no one there to let him in? What if he's hungry? Or hurt?"

"We can't go home," my father said. "Not yet anyway. The roof needs to be replaced. The wiring is wet, so there's no electricity, and the whole place reeks of smoke. All the carpeting and bedding and curtains will have to be cleaned or thrown out. That's how . . ."

His voice trailed off before he'd finished the sentence.

"That's how what?" I asked.

"Your mom wanted to strip the beds to see if the mattresses could be saved, and . . ." He hesitated again and looked over at my mother, who was still standing in the hall.

"Take off your coat, Ruby," he said. "You're dripping on the rug."

My mother didn't move, and her face was still as pond water.

"What's wrong?" I asked.

"We need to talk, Aurora," my mother said.

"About what?"

She reached into her pocket and pulled out the Zippo lighter.

"About this."

CHAPTER EIGHT

More than a finger loves to point

"What's the big deal?" I asked, rubbing my forehead with the knuckle of my right thumb, something new I had started doing recently. "It's just a dumb old lighter. I forgot I even had it."

My father had finally managed to convince my mother to take off her coat, and the two of them were sitting next to each other on the living room couch. I sat across from them in a wooden chair, wearing the same nightgown I'd had on the night before, when the fire started. One of the boys, Joe or Jack, wandered out of his room bleary-eyed, in flip-flops and a pair of giant basketball shorts. He disappeared into the bathroom, and a minute later we heard the shower running.

"Where did it come from?" my mother asked.

"I found it in the grass by the mailbox."

"When?" she asked.

"What difference does it make?"

"I'm just trying to understand," she said.

"Understand what?"

"Why did you hide the lighter under your mattress?" my father asked. "Why didn't you tell us about it? It's not like you to keep secrets."

"Why didn't you tell me there was something wrong with your heart?" I shot back.

"Because a murmur isn't a big deal," my father said.

"Neither is the lighter," I insisted.

"Then why did you hide it?" my mother asked.

"Because I knew you guys wouldn't let me keep it. Especially you, Mom. Everybody knows what a worrywart you are."

"A *worrywart*?" my mother said.

"That's what Uncle James called you."

"Well, Uncle James should mind his own business," my mother snapped, color rising in her cheeks. "He doesn't know the first thing about raising a child."

"Do you?" I asked.

"What's that supposed to mean?" my mother said, and I could tell I'd hurt her feelings.

"I'm sure Rory didn't mean it the way it sounded," my father said.

I wasn't sure what I'd meant or why I'd said it. It just came out. Ever since I'd seen that photograph I'd felt confused, tangled up inside like the necklaces in my mother's jewelry box. I couldn't think straight, and it wasn't helping that my parents kept peppering me with questions about the lighter.

"What in the world would you even want with an old lighter like that?" my father asked.

"Didn't you ever find something cool when you were a kid and want to keep it?" I asked back.

He nodded. "Arrowheads and bottle caps."

"This is not the same," my mother said, the color in her cheeks rising even higher. "Roy, tell her it's not the same thing."

"Why are you making such a stink, Mom? It's just a dumb old lighter. (A) It doesn't even work, and (B) try it for yourself, if you don't believe me."

Without a word, my mother flipped open the top, *svvvit!* Then she pressed her thumb against the little wheel and pushed down. There was a click, followed by a spark. A yellow flame rose up.

"Give her a chance to explain, Rube."

"Explain what?" I asked. I felt my own cheeks growing hot.

"Let's everybody calm down," my father said.

"I am calm," I told him. "You guys are the ones who are acting weird."

"Were you upset about the chest?" my mother asked. "Is that what it was?"

"Why would I be upset about the chest, Mom? I helped Dad keep the secret, remember?"

"You said you wished it was yours. You said you wanted to use it for your summer clothes in the winter and your winter clothes in the—"

"What does that have to do with anything?" I interrupted.

My mother looked at my father.

"Roy?" she pleaded as the first tear rolled down her cheek. "I need your help."

My father stood up and cleared his throat. Something was coming.

"When your mother found the lighter, she was afraid—we were both afraid that you might have . . ."

"What?" I asked, alarmed.

"Sometimes when people are very upset or their feelings are hurt they do things they regret later on," my mother explained. "Bad things."

What was she talking about? What bad thing did she think I had done?

Suddenly it dawned on me.

"You think I set the fire," I said.

"Did you?" my mother asked softly.

I felt like my head was about to explode.

"Are you *crazy*?" I cried, jumping out of my chair so fast it fell back with a clatter. "Do you think I wanted Duck to run away too?"

"Of course not," my mother said. "We're just trying to understand."

"Understand what? Why I would set the house on fire and scare away the only friend I've ever had?"

"Let's everybody calm down," my father said again.

"No!" I yelled at him. "I don't want to calm down!"

"Get ahold of yourself, Aurora," he said.

"Get ahold of your own self," I told him. "She's accusing me of setting the fire, Dad."

"It's not just me," my mother said quietly.

I turned and looked at my father.

"You don't really think I would do that, do you, Dad?"

He looked down at his shoes.

"I don't know what to think," he said.

"Great. Well then, the two of you can stay here and think horrible things about me. I'm going home to look for Duck, and don't you dare try to stop me."

I snatched my father's yellow slicker off the hook in the hall and bolted out the front door, into the pouring rain. I wasn't sure which way to go, so I just started running. I didn't get very far before my father pulled up beside me in the car and rolled down the window.

"Hop in," he called out.

I was barefoot, and the slicker was way too big for me. The rain was coming down in sheets now, hitting my face at an angle, the way Lindsey's hand had smacked the rubber ball on the playground.

"Please, Rory," my father begged. "Get in the car."

I probably wouldn't have made it home on my own anyway, especially without shoes on, but I wasn't about to give up without a fight.

"I'm only getting in if you take me back to the house to look for Duck."

He reached across the seat and unlatched the door for me.

"Promise?" I said.

"Promise."

I climbed in, and my father turned the heater on full blast. Even so, it took a while before my teeth stopped chattering. I started to rub my forehead with my knuckle, but I had done it so many times already that morning that it was sore. I tapped the edge of the seat instead.

"Your mom picked up some clothes and a pair of shoes for you earlier, when we were over at the house," my father said, pushing a plastic bag across the seat toward me. "They might smell a little smoky, but at least they're dry."

I wasn't about to change in front of my father. Besides, anything I put on was only going to get wet anyway. I was grateful for the shoes and socks though. My feet felt like a couple of Popsicles.

"Rory," my father began, "about what just happened back there—"

I cut him off before he could go any further.

"(A) I don't want to talk about what just happened, and (B) if you try to make me talk about it, I'm going to jump out of this car right now. Got it?"

"Got it," my father said. "Okay if I turn the radio on?"

I shrugged.

We didn't sing along this time. As far as I was concerned, until we found Duck there wouldn't be anything worth singing about.

CHAPTER NINE

More than a key loves to turn

The house looked like a giant loaf of bread wrapped in a plastic bag. The middle of the roof was caved in, half the windows were busted out, and the yard looked like a herd of buffalo had stampeded through it.

"Duck!" I called, hopping out of the car before my father had even turned the engine off. "Here, boy!"

My mother's gardening hat lay upside down in a muddy puddle now, and the reindeer ornament had come unglued and fallen completely to pieces, the little red pom-pom I'd used for the nose squashed flat and blackened with soot.

"Duck!" I called again.

My father joined me, and together we walked around the yard and through the field behind the house, whistling and calling Duck's name until our throats were raw. After about an hour of searching we circled back.

"We need to get going, Rory," my father said. "Your mother will be worried."

I didn't care if she was worried . . . and I was still a little mad at my father too, for that matter. He should have stuck up for me.

"I'm not going back," I said. "Not until we find Duck."

We must have walked up and down our road ten times, flagging down every passing car to ask if they had seen a black dog with a red collar. I can only imagine what people thought when they saw me in that giant yellow slicker, my muddy nightgown hanging out the bottom, shouting and waving my arms. Everybody stopped, a few even offered to help search, but nobody had seen Duck.

Cold, wet, and discouraged, we finally climbed back into the car without him.

By that time I was finding it hard to stay mad at my father.

"What if we never find him?" I asked as we started back down the driveway.

"That would be very sad," he answered. "But we could get another dog."

"I don't want another dog!" I said, fighting back tears. "I want Duck!"

He reached over and patted my knee.

"I know, honey," he said. "But sometimes no matter how much you want something, it isn't meant to be."

"He has to be out there somewhere," I said.

"It's possible someone has found him. If so, I'm sure they're taking good care of him. We'll keep looking and calling the shelter, but there isn't much more we can do here, baby girl. Not right now."

I pushed his hand away and leaned my head against the window. There was something I wanted to ask him, something that had been bothering me since I'd found the photograph in my mother's jewelry box.

"Do you feel the same way about Heidi as Mom does?"

There was a clap of thunder, and a bright yellow zipper of lightning split the sky. The windshield started fogging up, and my father used his hand to wipe it off.

"Your mom and Heidi are very close," he said. "They have a special kind of bond."

"Do you?"

"What's this all about, kiddo?" my father asked.

"Can you please just answer the question?" I asked him.

He paused for a moment. The rain beating on the roof of the car sounded like applause.

"Heidi was a sweet young girl when she came here," he said finally, "but to be honest, I don't know her very well now. Your mother is the one who's kept in touch."

"Did you want Heidi to stay and live with you as much as Mom did?"

"Sure," he said. "We thought maybe she would have a better life with us here."

"But she wanted to go home and live with Bernadette instead, right?"

"Mmm-hmm." My father nodded. "Your mother took it pretty hard when things didn't work out, but then you came along and we lived happily every after."

Suddenly I was so mad I could spit.

"Blah, blah, blah!" I said, kicking the dashboard with my muddy shoes.

"Hey!" my father said. "You're not a baby. Use words."

"*Blah* is a word," I said.

"Well, find some better ones to tell me why you're so upset, and put your feet down on the floor where they belong—you know better than that."

I did as he told me and took my feet off the dashboard. But I was still mad.

"How can you say that we lived happily ever after when Duck is still missing and you and Mom think I set the house on fire?" I said. "Some fairy tale."

He turned and looked me straight in the eye.

"Were you telling the truth when you said you thought the lighter didn't work?"

"Cross my heart and hope to die."

"You don't need to say that," he told me.

"I didn't set the fire, Dad. I swear. It must have been a mouse chewing through a wire or something. Like Chief Strauss said. I didn't do it, Dad. You have to believe me."

I rubbed my forehead with my knuckle, even though it hurt.

"Stop," he said, grabbing my hand and squeezing it tight. "I believe you."

"Promise?"

"Promise."

"Well, Mom still thinks I did it," I said.

"I'll talk to your mother," he told me. "Don't worry—she'll come around."

We stopped at McDonald's on the way home, but my father swore me to secrecy.

"You know how your mother feels about fast food," he

said as he dipped a french fry into a puddle of ketchup and wolfed it down.

I locked my lips and threw away the imaginary key.

When we got back to Scott and Julie's house, my mother met us at the door.

"Any luck?" she asked. "And please tell me that's not ketchup I see on your cuff, Roy Franklin."

He gave her a lopsided grin.

"Sorry, Rube," he told her. "We were hungry, and no, we didn't find Duck."

My mother tried to get me to sit down with her. She wanted to talk about what had happened, but I was all talked out.

"Let her be," my father said, putting his arm around Mom. "She's had a long day. How about you put on a pot of coffee and I'll fill you in?"

"How about you make the coffee?" she said. "I've had a long day too."

I went straight to my room to change out of my wet things. My mother had been busy. The bed was made, and there was a pile of freshly laundered clothes sitting on the sewing table. As usual my mother had turned all the shirts inside out for me before she'd folded them. After changing into a T-shirt and a pair of flannel pajama pants, I lay down on the soggy air mattress and crawled under the covers. It was still light out, too early to go to bed, but I was exhausted. Every time I started drifting off, though, the image of that photograph of my mother with her arms around Heidi came back to me. What was it I had seen in her eyes? The rain had finally stopped and the wind picked up, rattling the windows and blowing through the branches of the trees outside my window.

Soof, they whispered. *Soof.*

I must have slept for a long time, because when I woke up it was dark out and the whole house was quiet. I felt a little hungry and went out to the kitchen to get a snack. When I opened the fridge a wedge of cold yellow light spilled across the counter, catching in the clasp of my mother's jewelry box. It was exactly where I'd left it. My stomach rumbled like a train in a tunnel, but I ignored it.

Leaving the refrigerator door ajar so I could see, I opened the lid and took out the photograph.

Everyone was asleep. I had all the time in the world, but it didn't take long for me to figure it out. The trees outside my window had been trying to tell me. They knew the truth, and now so did I.

There was no doubt about it. The look in my mother's eyes was definitely *soof*.

CHAPTER TEN

More than a clock loves to tick

The sun was shining brightly the next morning when I woke up, but the weather didn't match my dark mood. All night long I had tossed and turned, thinking about the photograph. How could my mother have told me that story about Heidi passing her luck along when she knew that it wasn't true? Luck had nothing to do with my being born. Heidi was the child she'd been waiting for all her life, not me.

I propped myself up on my elbows and stared out the window. The trees were quiet now, having passed their message along. Duck wasn't getting rained on wherever he was, so at least there was that to be grateful for. I glanced at the clock. It was seven thirty. Hopefully some-one would be answering at the animal shelter in Rock Hill. We'd had Duck microchipped when we got him, but the phone number on his collar was the landline at our house, and who knew if the answering machine was even working anymore?

The nearest phone was in the living room. When I got there I found my mother and Julie sitting on the couch together. Julie was knitting and my mother was working on the baby quilt for Heidi, which she must have brought back with her from the house. I felt a flash of anger. No wonder she'd saved the curtains from the room where Heidi had slept; everything that had anything to do with her was special.

"Good morning, Aurora," my mother said. "Did you sleep well, sweetie?"

"Why do you care?" I muttered. Then I headed for the kitchen, where I knew there was another phone. I got the number for the shelter from information, but nobody picked up, so I couldn't even leave a message. Having slept through dinner, I was starved. I poured myself a big bowl of cereal—Lucky Charms this time—and carried it back to my room. The air mattress must have had a slow leak, because it looked like an ice-cream sandwich that had been left out in the sun. I ate the cereal standing up, taking a certain amount of pleasure in knowing that my mother would disapprove. We didn't have junk like Froot Loops or Lucky Charms at our house. Instead my mother would make granola from scratch, chopping up all kinds of nuts and dried fruit and mixing them together in a big bowl of rolled oats along with some coconut oil and honey. I scooped up the last bite of cereal and drank the sugary pink milk from the bottom of the bowl.

So there, I thought.

There was a knock on the door.

"Leave me alone," I grumbled.

"It's Julie, hon. I need to get some yarn."

"Sorry about that," I said, hurrying to open the door for her. "I thought you were somebody else."

"Oh my goodness," she said when she saw the deflated air mattress. "We can't have you sleeping on that. I'll have Scott patch it up as soon as he gets home." She paused for a second and looked around the room. "Did you reorganize these shelves or something? Everything looks so . . . tidy."

"I hope you don't mind," I told her. "I evened things up a little and switched out some of the tops so there would be the same number of each color on every shelf."

"Well, bless your heart," said Julie.

I watched while she dug around in one of the bins until she found what she was after—a ball of bright red yarn and another one of white.

"I thought I'd make you guys some new Christmas stockings," she explained. "Your mom told me the holiday stuff was up in the attic. What a shame to lose all those memories."

I'd been so busy thinking about Duck, I hadn't thought about what else we might have lost in the fire. Christmas was a big deal in our family. On the first Saturday of December, my father and I would get in the truck and drive over to Krasner's Farm. Once we'd found the perfect tree, my father would kneel down beside it and drag the saw over the trunk a few times, like a violinist drawing his bow across the strings. Once the saw blade bit into the bark and took hold, I'd grab onto the other end and we'd find our rhythm pushing and pulling back and forth, until finally the tree gave up and fell back onto the snow like a fainting woman in a big green ball gown. We'd throw our prize in the back of the truck along with a balsam wreath for the front door and drive home to my mother, who would be waiting with hot chocolate and gingerbread cookies.

My mother was pretty crafty all year-round, but she really outdid herself at Christmas. Every year she'd make a new kind of ornament. There were flocks of crocheted birds perched on cinnamon sticks and delicate wreaths of eucalyptus leaves, each one carefully tied with a red ribbon. One year she saved the wishbones from every chicken we ate, lining them up on the kitchen windowsill to dry. After she'd painted them silver, she glued little glass beads to the top of each one for the hooks to go through. Those were my favorites. Hanging from the tips of the branches, they caught the light, glimmering like little wishes waiting to be made.

Unlike my mother, I was not crafty at all. For one thing, I hated getting my fingers sticky. I was also not fond of glitter, but each year at school we made ornaments in art class, and my mother had saved every single one. There were cut-paper snowflakes, a giant pinecone half-heartedly dusted with green glitter, several snowmen made out of pipe cleaners, and the lopsided Popsicle stick reindeer that had ended up in pieces after the fire.

Julie was staring at me.

"Are you okay, hon?" she asked. "You look like you're a million miles away."

"Sorry," I said. "I was just thinking."

Julie started to leave, but then she hesitated.

"I know it's none of my business," she said, "but your mother's really hurting right now. She's been crying all morning. I think it would help if you could sit down and talk to her."

I felt another spark of irritation, this one even hotter.

"Did she tell you she thinks I set the house on fire?" I asked.

Julie looked uncomfortable.

"She overreacted. She doesn't believe that anymore, Aurora. You have to understand she was upset when she found the lighter. You know how she worries. Believe it or not it was even worse when you were a baby. Your mother recorded every sneeze and burp in that journal of hers."

Julie wasn't exaggerating. I'd discovered the journal on a shelf in the living room one day. It was a small square book with a weathered blue cover and a thin satin ribbon sewn into the spine to use as a placeholder. *BABY'S FIRST YEAR* was embossed on the cover in gold.

The first few pages were filled with details about the day I was born, including a tiny plastic wristband from the hospital with *Baby girl, Franklin* printed on it. There was a list of names my parents had considered before Heidi had suggested they call me Aurora. Next came a long list of milestones, each with two dates written beside it. One when I had done it and one when I was *supposed* to have done it according to one of the many baby books she'd kept stacked beside the bed.

I had not been an easy baby. Because I had colic, my mother spent most of her time worrying about what went in one end of me and what came out the other. My father wasn't much help—not because he didn't care, but because he wasn't around. This left my mother alone with a fussy baby and no one there to tell her not to fret. Ironically, most of the worrying she did had taken place in a big oak rocking chair, which still sat in a corner of our living room. She rocked and worried and poured her heart out onto the pages of her journal, which carried her like a weathered blue boat through the rough seas of her baby's first year.

Julie left with her yarn.

"Hey," I called after her. "Do you know where my dad is?"

I wanted to ask him if he'd heard anything from the shelter in Rock Hill.

"He's at work, hon," Julie said. "Left about an hour ago."

Great. What was I supposed to do, hang around the house all day trying to avoid my mother? Something occurred to me.

"Why's he working on a Sunday?" I asked.

Julie gave me a funny look.

"Today is Monday, hon."

"Monday?" I looked at the clock. It still said seven thirty. I hadn't noticed the cord dangling off the side of the table, unplugged. "What time is it for real?" I asked.

Julie looked at her watch.

"Half past nine," she said.

So much for my perfect attendance record. I was late for school.

CHAPTER ELEVEN

More than an ear loves to listen

I barely spoke to my mother on the drive to school. When I asked her why she hadn't woken me up at 6:45 the way she usually did on weekdays, she explained that she'd assumed that, under the circumstances, I wouldn't want to go.

"Under the circumstances, you assumed wrong," I told her, giving my nose three quick taps. "In case you forgot, which you obviously did, I've got a perfect attendance record. At least I used to. Now, thanks to you, I have a big fat tardy." Tap, tap, tap.

"I'm sorry, sweetie," my mother said. "I guess I should have asked. I can speak to Mr. Taylor, if you'd like. I'm sure he'll understand."

The truth was, I didn't really care about messing up my attendance record. Compared with everything else that was going on, it seemed pretty trivial.

"(A) I don't need you to talk to Mr. Taylor. I need you to leave me alone. And (B) don't call me sweetie anymore."

"Aurora," my mother said, her eyes brimming with fresh tears, "I know that you're angry at me about what happened yesterday. I didn't mean to hurt your feelings."

"Blah, blah, blah," I said and put my hands over my ears. "Blah, blah, blah, blah, blah."

We drove the rest of the way in silence, except for my mother's sniffling. She could cry all she wanted, as far as I was concerned. She had lied to me my whole life, and I had a right to be mad about that.

* * *

Mr. Taylor made a big fuss when I walked into class. He explained that they'd had a special assembly first thing that morning to discuss what had happened to my family over the weekend.

"Your classmates and I were wondering if there's anything we can do to help," he told me.

"Do you need food?" Brian Tucker asked. "We've got a whole ham in the freezer at home. Nobody in my family likes ham, so I can ask my mom if you guys could have it. There might be a frozen lasagna in there too."

I was pretty sure Brian Tucker had never actually spoken to me before, let alone offered me a frozen ham.

"No thanks," I said. "We're staying with some family friends in North Branch, and they've got plenty of food. I had Lucky Charms for breakfast."

"I like those too," said Brian.

"Did you get burned in the fire?" asked Kristie Minor, one of the girls who'd been playing foursquare on the playground the day I'd found Lindsey's silver charm.

"'Cause my uncle did once, and they had to take some skin off his butt and put it on his face."

Everyone started laughing, and Mr. Taylor clapped his hands.

"This is no laughing matter," he said to the class. "Imagine if this had happened to you. Imagine if you had lost your home and all your belongings."

The room was silent.

"I'm sorry, Aurora," said Kristie. "I wasn't trying to be funny."

Lindsey Toffle raised her hand.

"Do you have a question?" Mr. Taylor asked.

"Actually, it's a comment," she said. "My father was one of the firemen who put out the fire. I'm pretty sure he was the first one there, so I guess that makes him kind of a hero."

I thought about the way Lindsey's father had spoken to me when I'd asked him if they'd found Duck. *We didn't find any dog.* That's when it occurred to me: There was something I did need help with. Something really important.

"I need to make some flyers," I said. "To put up around town. My dog, Duck, ran away after the fire, and I'm trying to find him."

"Do you have a photo of your dog that we can put on the flyers?" asked Mr. Taylor.

I shook my head.

"I have lots of pictures at home, but we're not allowed to go in the house right now without permission from the fire chief."

"I guess that means the flyers will need to have drawings on them instead of a photograph," said Mr. Taylor.

I nodded.

"What do you think, friends?" he asked the class. "Shall we help Aurora make some flyers?"

A cheer went up, and so did Lindsey's hand.

"Will you be offering a reward?" she asked.

I hadn't thought about that. My piggy bank was completely empty. I'd spent the last of my allowance on Duck's red collar and a matching leash.

"What about the ham?" Brian suggested.

"Nobody wants your stupid ham," snarled Lindsey. "They're going to want money."

"Mr. Taylor?" I said. "Are you going to mark me tardy for today?"

Mr. Taylor shook his head.

"Today doesn't count," he said. "We're glad you're here. Don't worry, your record still stands."

"Thanks," I said. "But the reason I was asking is because I think maybe a cherry pie would make a good reward for finding Duck."

Mr. Taylor smiled.

"Jickity-jack, that's a stellar idea," he said.

Out of the corner of my eye I saw Lindsey make a face. She'd been trying to suck up to Mr. Taylor all year, and it never seemed to work.

"Can you describe your dog for us, please, Aurora?" Mr. Taylor asked as he handed out sheets of white paper and markers to everyone.

"He's all black with a red collar," I said. "He weighs sixty-two pounds, and the inside of his ears smells like popcorn."

Lindsey rolled her eyes. "How are we supposed to draw *that*?"

"She didn't say you had to draw it, Lindsey," commented Kristie. "She's just telling us what Duck is like, right, Aurora?"

It was hard for me to wrap my head around the fact that Kristie Minor was actually taking my side against Lindsey Toffle.

"Yeah," I said. "I guess so."

There weren't enough black and red markers to go around, so some people drew green dogs with blue collars or orange dogs with pink collars instead. For some reason Stephanie Morris drew a unicorn jumping over a rainbow on her flyer, but Mr. Taylor made her throw it away and start over. Everyone in the class made at least one flyer. Lindsey's was one of the best. She drew Duck in the foreground, looking over his shoulder at a house with bright orange flames shooting out of the windows. Somehow she managed to actually make him look worried.

"Thanks," I said when she showed it to me. "It's really good."

"I know," she told me. "That's why I'm probably going to keep it, and not put it up. It might get ruined if it rains."

"Oh," I said. "Okay."

"You can borrow my charm bracelet if you want though. Not to take home, I mean to wear for a little while. You'll have to wash your hands first though, and you can't touch any of the charms or drop it, or drag it across your desk, because it's fragile. You remember what happened before."

"I remember," I said.

But I didn't want to borrow her stupid bracelet. All I cared about was finding Duck.

"Friends," Mr. Taylor said, when we were finished drawing, "part two of this project is to take your flyers home this afternoon and hang them up where people will be sure to see them."

I looked at Lindsey to see if she was listening, but she was busy playing with her bracelet.

At lunch, Joanne Kriskowsky asked if she could sit next to me.

"You can have half my sandwich, if you want," she said.

In our rush to leave the house that morning, my mother had forgotten to pack me a lunch, and I didn't have money to buy a hot lunch. Other kids kept coming over and offering me food too. Brian Tucker even gave me his Fruit Roll-Up.

I knew I should have been grateful to everybody for being so nice to me, but I didn't feel grateful—I felt nervous. I was used to eating lunch alone. I couldn't think of anything to say, so I sat there tapping and scratching and jiggling my legs under the table. After lunch, when everyone finally went outside to the playground, I hurried down the hall to Mrs. Strawgate's office.

"Aurora!" she said, jumping up from her chair when she saw me. "I'm so glad you stopped by. I've been thinking about you."

She asked me a bunch of questions about the fire and about how I was feeling. I liked Mrs. Strawgate—she always had real flowers in her office, and she was a good listener. But the reason I had come to see her now was because I had a question of my own.

"What's the difference between a secret and a lie?" I asked.

She thought about it for a minute.

"That's a very interesting question," she said. "Off the top of my head I would say a secret is something private that you keep to yourself, and a lie is something you tell someone else even though you know it isn't true."

"What if somebody does both—keeps a secret and tells you a lie? What's that called?"

"Complicated," she said.

I couldn't concentrate in class that afternoon, so Mr. Taylor told me it would be okay if I wanted to skip my lessons and work on making more flyers instead.

Sometimes when I was really focusing on something, I made sounds with my tongue—clicking and clucking. I didn't realize I was doing it, but when a couple of kids complained that I was distracting them during silent reading, Lindsey Toffle took it upon herself to ask Mr. Taylor if he could please move my desk out into the hall. He smiled politely and told her that if she was having trouble getting her work done, she was free to move her own desk out into the hall.

Some of my previous teachers would get annoyed with me when I couldn't sit still in class. Knowing that they were watching made me even jumpier. Mr. Taylor wasn't like that. He kept a basket of fidget spinners on his desk. Kids were allowed to borrow them whenever they wanted, and sometimes Mr. Taylor even used one himself.

Before we left that afternoon, Mr. Taylor told us that our only homework assignment for the night was to put up the flyers.

"Jickity-jack, let's bring Duck home!" he said, and everyone whooped and hollered.

Even though I was worried about Duck, and mad at my mother and basically feeling pretty bummed out in general, it made me feel good to see people putting those flyers into their homework folders. Maybe, just maybe one of them would do the trick.

My mother wasn't there yet when I got outside, so I sat down on the curb to wait. Twenty minutes later, she finally showed up.

"Sorry I'm late," she told me. "I had to pick out new shingles for the roof, and it took longer than I expected. How was school?"

I shrugged. "We made flyers to help find Duck."

"That's wonderful," she said.

We drove for a while in silence. Then to my surprise, my mother pulled into the Dairy Queen and turned off the engine.

"Do you have homework to do this afternoon? Because I was thinking maybe we could both use some ice cream," she said. "My treat."

"Mom, I'm not stupid," I told her. "(A) We both know the only reason you want to take me out for ice cream is so that we can talk, and (B) I don't want to talk to you. I want to put up flyers. That's it. The end. No more."

"Suit yourself," my mother said, "but I'm going to grab a butterscotch sundae for the road. I'll be right back."

Since she was getting ice cream anyway, I decided I might as well get a Dilly Bar. There was no drive-through, so my mother suggested we eat our ice cream inside instead of in the car. The guy behind the counter was slower than a snail, and even though our order was pretty simple, he messed up twice.

"Thanks for the ice cream," I said to my mother as we sat down opposite each other in a booth. "But this doesn't mean we're going to talk."

"Okay," she said. Then she plucked the cherry off the top of her sundae and popped it in her mouth.

On the way in I had noticed a bulletin board covered with ads and notices about yard sales and penny socials happening around town. When I had finished my ice cream and washed my hands in the restroom, I went out to the car to get one of my flyers so I could put it up. Lots of people came to the Dairy Queen. Maybe one of them would have seen Duck.

My mother kept her promise and didn't talk to me while we were eating, other than to ask if I wanted another Dilly Bar, which I didn't. As we were getting back in the car, her cell phone buzzed. It was a text from Julie, and when she was finished reading, her eyes were sparkling.

"I guess one of those flyers of yours must have worked," she told me. "Julie says she just got a call."

My heart leapt.

"About Duck?" I cried.

She nodded.

"Let's go get your dog."

CHAPTER TWELVE

More than a tail loves to wag

"Beep-beep-boppity-bip kapow!" I crowed.

"No translation necessary." My mother laughed. "I may not be fluent in Beepish, but I'm pretty sure that means you're happy Duck is coming home."

"How much farther?" I asked.

"It's over on the other side of town. We should be there in about ten minutes."

I couldn't believe it. Only ten minutes until I could hug Duck. Ten minutes until I could kiss his head and sniff his ears and man oh man, does ten minutes feel like a million years when you can't wait to see your dog.

"Put the pedal to the metal!" I cried happily.

My mother laughed again.

"Where in the world did you pick up that expression?" she asked.

"Mr. Taylor says it all the time. He also says *get the lead out, jumpin' Jehosaphat, holy Toledo,* and *jickity-jack.*"

"Jickity-jack?"

"I don't know exactly what it means," I said, "but it's definitely a good thing."

My mother smiled.

"Mr. Taylor is a good thing too, isn't he?"

"He's the best teacher in the whole world," I gushed. "He doesn't make me join in if I don't want, he lets me color in all the *o*'s on the bulletin boards, and today he told Lindsey Toffle she could sit out in the hall her own self if she didn't like the sounds I was making."

"What sounds were you making?" my mother asked, glancing over at me.

"Nothing you haven't heard before. We must be almost there by now. Can't you drive any faster?"

My mother ignored the question and kept the speed-ometer steady at fifty-five.

"It's good to be talking again," she said. "I've missed you."

"*Mom*," I moaned. "Not now."

I was finally feeling happy about something—did she have to ruin it with some corny blibbity blabbing about missing me?

"Please hear me out," my mother insisted. "I have to get this off my chest."

"Fine," I said, crossing my arms and heaving a giant sigh. "I'm listening."

"I feel awful about what I said to you after I found the lighter," my mother began. "I know you would never have done anything to put our family in danger. It was a terrible thing for me to say, and I'm beyond sorry."

I knew I was supposed to say that I forgave her, or that it was okay, or not to worry . . . but as awful as I'd felt when she accused me of setting the fire, it wasn't the main thing I was mad at her about. If I said that I forgave her, it would feel like I was forgiving her for everything. I wasn't ready to do that, and I didn't know if I ever would be.

"If you say so," I told her instead.

It was clear that wasn't the response she'd been hoping for, but it was the best I could do under the circumstances. A few minutes later, we slowed down, pulled off the highway, and turned up a narrow dirt road. The houses were small and close together, the yards full of weeds and plastic toys.

"Julie's text said fifty-four Bryer Road, but do you see any numbers on these houses?" my mother asked, craning her neck to see.

"There it is!" I shouted, pointing to a green house with some faded numbers peeling off the side of the mailbox. There was an old car up on cinder blocks in the driveway, and a snowmobile with a *FOR SALE* sign on it parked in the middle of the front yard. I looked around, but there was no sign of Duck.

"Let me check again, to make sure we're in the right place," my mother said, but before she could pull up the text on her phone, the screen door banged open and a skinny woman smoking a cigarette stepped out. She had on short shorts and a tank top with a big red tongue printed on it.

"You the folks that lost a dog?" she called out to us.

"Is he okay?" I asked, jumping out of the car. "He's not hurt, is he?"

"Looks fine to me. My husband caught him digging in the garbage this morning. Probably after the chicken bones I chucked in there last night."

Poor Duck. He must have been hungry after three days out on his own. I would feed him something really nice for dinner—maybe some of those special hot dogs Julie had mentioned.

"We're so glad you called," my mother said. "We've been worried sick about him. You see, our house caught fire the other night, and—"

"Where is he?" I interrupted. "Where's Duck?"

"He's tied up around back," she said, pointing with the hand that was holding the cigarette. It left a little trail of smoke behind it, like one of those planes that writes messages in the sky.

As I rounded the corner of the house and caught sight of his wagging tail, I felt like my heart was about to burst right out of my chest.

"Duck!" I shouted. "Duck!"

He let out a happy bark, turned around, and ran toward me as far as the rope would allow. Only it wasn't Duck. This dog was mangy and old, his teeth were yellow, and instead of a red collar there was a dirty bandana tied around his neck.

I felt like I'd been punched in the stomach.

"Guess we better call the shelter then," the skinny woman said when she found out the dog wasn't ours. "Somebody must be looking for him."

"Why did this have to happen?" I wailed as we drove away from the green house, empty-handed. "I feel like I've lost Duck all over again."

"I know, sweetie," my mother said. "I feel the same way."

"No, you don't," I sobbed. "You don't know anything about how I feel. It's my fault he's gone."

"It isn't your fault Duck ran away," my mother said. "It isn't anyone's fault."

I shook my head.

"I should have made sure that he was with us when we left the house."

"You mustn't blame yourself," she said. "You were frightened. We all were. Nobody was thinking straight."

I covered my face with my hands and moaned.

"We never should have made those stupid flyers. The drawings don't even look like Duck. There weren't enough markers, so the colors aren't right."

"We can get more markers," my mother said. "As many as you need. We'll go to the store right now."

"You don't get it, Mom. Markers aren't going to fix anything. We need a photograph. But I don't have any pictures of Duck. They're all in the house, or maybe they're burned up, gone forever like everything else I ever cared about."

My tears were flowing hot and heavy now, and it felt like a giant hand was squeezing my middle. Suddenly, without warning, my mother jammed on the brakes so hard I might have gone right through the windshield if I hadn't been buckled in.

"What are you doing?" I cried.

"We're going back."

"To Scott and Julie's?"

"No," she said, turning the car around so fast the tires squealed. "We're going home."

CHAPTER THIRTEEN

More than a broom loves to sweep

"Are we going to get in trouble?" I asked as my mother unlocked the front door.

"No," she said, stepping inside. "We came into the house once before, and as long as we don't go upstairs, I don't see any reason why we can't be here now. They've already started work on the roof, and it's still completely covered. Besides, we're not planning to stay long."

There were dark streaks of soot on the walls. Plaster peeled from the ceiling where it had gotten wet.

"What's that awful smell?" I asked, wrinkling my nose.

"Mildew," my mother said. "And smoke. It's going to be a big job cleaning this mess up."

My room looked pretty much the same as it had before the fire except for the dirty walls and a broken window, which had been covered up with a sheet of plywood. The black dots where I'd tapped with the broom handle were still on the ceiling, but the covers had been stripped off the bed and sent to the cleaners. There was a pink sock lying on the mattress—the one I had put the lighter inside before I'd hidden it. That seemed like a million years ago. So much had happened since then—none of it good.

There were several pictures of Duck pinned to the bulletin board over my desk. Luckily none of them had been harmed. I couldn't decide which one would be best for the flyer, so I took them all down and went out to the kitchen to find a plastic bag to put them in.

My mother was standing on a step stool, removing the kitchen curtains.

"Did you find what you needed?" she asked as she unhooked the last ring and tossed the curtains into a wicker laundry basket along with her yellow apron and a bunch of dish towels, all of which she planned to wash later at Scott and Julie's. Duck's rug—the one he always slept on—was lying on the floor. I picked it up and handed it to my mother.

"We need to wash this too," I said. "For when he comes home."

She nodded and put it in the basket.

After we'd thrown everything in the car I asked my mother to wait while I went around back and whistled for Duck in case he was nearby.

"Here, boy!" I called. "Here, Duck!" But the only response I got was a raspy scolding from a blue jay watching from a nearby tree.

If there was a silver lining to be found in my sorry situation, it was that Heidi would no longer be coming to visit. We couldn't very well have company when we didn't even have a house to have company in. I was relieved that I wouldn't have to share my room with her, but mostly I was relieved that I wouldn't have to meet her. Knowing what I knew now about my mother's feelings about her, I would be happy never to have to lay eyes on her at all.

The next morning, Julie helped me make a new flyer, using one of the photographs I'd brought back from the house. It was a picture I'd taken of Duck the day I'd bought his red collar. We made a bunch of copies at the library, and that evening after my father got home from work, he and I drove all around Liberty, stapling and taping up flyers.

We got a grand total of three calls over the next few weeks, but they all turned out to be false alarms. I kept checking with the animal shelter until finally they asked me not to call anymore. They promised they would let me know if Duck showed up. My fifteen minutes of fame were over at school, and most of the kids had gone back to ignoring me. Kristie and Joanne were still trying to be nice, inviting me to sit with them at lunch if I wanted to, but I could never think of anything to say to them, and after a while they stopped saving me a seat. Every time I ran into Mrs. Strawgate in the hall, she'd remind me that her door was always open, but I didn't feel like talking to her either. One day Mr. Taylor taught us how to make book spine poetry, and after that I spent a lot of my time in the school library, pulling books off the shelves and stacking them up to make poems out of their titles. I even made one about Duck.

One Good Dog
A Wrinkle in Time
Out of My Mind
Wish

I had tried to find books with the word *Duck* in the title, but the only ones I could come up with were *The Ugly Duckling* and *Duck for President*, neither of which worked. While I'd been searching the shelves for my poems, I rediscovered The Boxcar Children series and checked out a whole stack. Those stories had been some of the very first chapter books I'd ever read, and there was something comforting about spending time with the Alden kids again, even though the boys seemed to have more than their share of the adventures while the girls stayed home and did dishes.

Scott had patched the leaky air mattress, so I'd been sleeping a little better. During the day, while I was at school, my mother spent her time over at our house, overseeing the parade of painters and carpenters who came and went like ants at a picnic. On weekends we would all go over there together, and while my parents worked on the house, I would look for Duck.

We stayed with Scott and Julie for a total of three weeks, and when we finally moved back home, things got a little better between my mother and me. It takes a lot of energy to stay mad at someone, even if you have a good reason. The house was coming together nicely; my room had a new window and a fresh coat of paint. The dots on the ceiling were gone. We were still waiting for some furniture to be delivered, including a new couch, and the carpet needed to be installed, but life was beginning to feel almost normal again. As normal as it could without Duck anyway.

Then one day my mother got another letter from Heidi.

"Good news," she said when she'd finished reading it. "Heidi will be here next Sunday!"

I couldn't believe my ears.

"Why is she still coming?" I said. "Didn't you tell her about the fire? We don't even have a couch for her to sit on."

"She won't mind if things aren't perfect," my mother told me. "And with the baby coming in July, it's pretty much now or never."

Never sounded just fine to me.

"I'm not sharing my room with her," I protested. "I don't even know her, and besides . . ."

"Besides what?" my mother asked.

"Bip-bam-bash boom," I said, pounding a fist into my palm.

"Translation, please," my mother said.

"You figure it out," I told her. Then I went to my room, slamming the door behind me.

The photos of Duck were back on the bulletin board, and my mother had made me a new pair of curtains with flowers and butterflies all over them. At first I had loved the way they looked, like a meadow hanging in my window. Now I wondered if she'd made them for me or if they were really for Heidi.

My father was late coming home that night, so my mother and I ate together at the kitchen table. I pushed a breaded chicken cutlet around my plate for a while, then asked to be excused so I could get started on my homework. We were reading *Esperanza Rising* in class. I was pretty sure Mr. Taylor had chosen the book especially for me, because Esperanza's house catches on fire in the story. Once upon a time I had wondered why so many books written for kids are about sad things, but now I understood that sometimes it helps to know that sad things happen to other people too, even if they're not real.

Later, as I was brushing my teeth, I heard my father come home. I rinsed out my toothbrush and walked down the hall to say hello. He was out in the living room with my mother, who was sitting in a chair with her back to me. She was cradling something in her arms, rocking it like a baby as she wept.

"Don't cry, Rube," my father told her, kneeling down beside her. "We can get another."

I held my breath as he reached for whatever it was she was holding.

"I don't want another," she said. "It won't be the same."

It wasn't until he stood up that I could see that he had Heidi's jelly bean jar in his hands. The fire had cracked the glass and melted the beans into a single gooey mass.

She was right. It wouldn't ever be the same.

That night, I had another dream about Duck. He was sound asleep on his rug in the kitchen. When I came in, he opened his eyes and wagged just the tip of his tail. I lay down beside him on the floor and put my arms around him, pressing my nose into one of his soft black ears. When I woke up I was hugging my pillow, and I swore I could still smell popcorn. I closed my eyes and tried to climb back into the dream, but it didn't work so I lay there crying in the dark instead.

There was an ache deep down inside me, like a bruise that wouldn't heal. Back when I was in kindergarten my mother had explained that the pains I felt in my stomach sometimes when I was at school were called homesickness. Only the home I'd been missing then was a little white house where a black dog with a red collar lived along with a handsome father in a big gray hat and a doting mother in a yellow apron who loved her daughter more than anyone else in the world. The little white house was still there, it even had a brand-new roof, but all the colors inside it were gone, because the family that used to live there didn't exist anymore.

CHAPTER FOURTEEN

More than a cat loves to scratch

It was the end of June when Heidi arrived. School was out by then and I was officially in sixth grade. Mr. Taylor had hugged me goodbye on the last day.

"Good luck, Aurora," he'd told me. "And don't be a stranger."

Normally I was champing at the bit for summer vacation to start, but I was going to miss Mr. Taylor, especially with things being the way they were at home and Heidi's visit right around the corner. I was dreading it.

I had never had a sleepover in my life, so the trundle bed in my room had never been used. My mother opened it up and put fresh sheets on it the day before Heidi was due to arrive. I didn't make any secret about my feelings.

"I'll sleep in the hammock if I have to," I said. "I'm not sharing my room with some stranger."

"Heidi's not a stranger," my mother insisted as she unfolded a pillowcase. "She's more like family."

"Whatever," I said and started picking at an old mosquito bite on the back of my knee.

"Please don't do that, sweetie. It might get infected."

"It's *my* knee, not yours," I said. "And stop calling me sweetie."

"Are you girls at it again?" my father asked. He'd been out in the yard mowing the lawn, and there were little bits of grass sticking to his neck and arms. "It's like living with a couple of alley cats, the way you two go after each other lately."

"I can't help it if Mom's being annoying," I told him.

"Aurora has just informed me that she plans to sleep in the hammock while Heidi is here, Roy," my mother said, brushing a strand of hair out of her eyes. "But of course I'm the one who's being annoying."

I felt sorry for my father, who'd been caught like a monkey in the middle trying to keep peace between my mother and me ever since I'd found out that Heidi was still coming. It drove me crazy the way she'd been fussing, planning all the meals in advance and making everything nice for her precious, perfect little Heidi.

"What's going on with you, baby girl?" my father asked me later that day, when my mother had gone off to the store to buy blueberries to make a crumble, since that was Heidi's favorite. "Is it my imagination, or is someone's nose a little out of joint?"

"What's that supposed to mean?" I asked, closing my book.

I was lying in the rope hammock in the backyard, reading *Houseboat Mystery*, number twelve in The Boxcar Children series.

"It's an expression my father used to use," he said. "If

a person is feeling a little jealous, you say their nose is out of joint."

"Why should I be jealous?" I asked, but I could feel myself blushing, because of course he was right.

"Oh, I don't know," he said. "Maybe because your mom is making such a fuss."

"She bought special toilet paper, Dad," I told him. "The soft kind."

My father laughed.

"Your mother goes a little overboard sometimes, but this is a special occasion."

"Not for me it isn't," I said. "I don't even know Heidi."

"Well, then I guess it's about time you did."

They could make me meet her. But they weren't going to make me like her. Never in a million years.

The next day my mother came into my room to ask if I wanted to go along with them to the airport in Newburgh to pick Heidi up. I had finished *Houseboat Mystery* and had decided to take a break from The Boxcar Children and read *Esperanza Rising* again. A lot of bad things happened to Esperanza in the story, including that she loses her father, but at least her mother didn't act like the queen of England was coming to visit the way mine had for the past two weeks.

"Why doesn't Heidi go visit her own family?" I grumbled.

Thurman Hill and Heidi's father, Elliot, had moved to Florida several years earlier, when Hilltop Home had closed.

My mother sat down on the end of my bed. I noticed she had put on makeup, and she was wearing a pair of shoes I didn't recognize.

"I know you're not happy about Heidi coming," she said, "but I hope you'll at least try to be polite. She's a very nice person, and this is an important trip for her."

"What's so important about it?" I asked.

"She wants to visit her mama before the baby comes."

I had been so intent on finding out what Heidi had written about me that I'd skimmed over the rest of that first letter she'd sent. It hadn't even occurred to me to wonder why she had decided to visit. Heidi's mama was buried in the cemetery just up the hill from our house. For the first time, I felt a little guilty about the way I'd been behaving.

"You sure you don't want to come?" my mother asked.

I shook my head, and went back to my book.

Around three o'clock that afternoon I heard a car coming up the driveway, but when my mother stuck her head in to tell me Heidi had arrived, I pretended to be taking a nap. I wasn't ready to meet her yet. After my mother closed the door, I actually did fall asleep, and once again I dreamed about Duck. This time it was winter. My father and I were at Krasner's Farm, cutting down a Christmas tree. Duck was running around, barking his head off, and then all of a sudden I saw him leap into this giant snowbank and disappear. I called his name again and again, and when he didn't come, I jumped into the snowbank after him.

After that, the dream got really weird. I was inside a strange world, made out of ice. The air was so cold, it hurt to breathe. My mother was there now too, wearing her yellow apron and holding the jelly bean jar in her arms. Suddenly I looked down and my hands were turning blue, and then my fingers started falling off one by one, shattering as they hit the ground, the way the windows of the house had broken during the fire. I was afraid if I stayed in the ice world, I might freeze to death, but I couldn't leave without Duck. "Come back!" I called. "Come back!"

"Rory, honey. Wake up."

My father was shaking me.

"Duck is still in the snow!" I cried, sitting up.

"It's only a dream, baby girl," my father said. "Only a bad dream."

I buried my face in his shirt, and he put his arms around me.

"I can't do this anymore," I whispered. "It hurts too much to be me."

Heidi's belly was so big and round it looked like she was hiding a beach ball under her shirt.

"It's nice to finally meet you in person, Aurora," she said when my father finally convinced me to come out and say hello. "Bernie and I have all your school photos stuck up on the fridge at her place. It's like we've been watching you grow up right there in the kitchen."

I told her it was nice to meet her too, even though it wasn't true. She had brought a loaf of banana bread that Bernadette had baked for us, and a giant pencil for me that said *RENO* on it. My heart was beating so hard I could hear it.

"What do you say, Aurora?" my father prompted.

"Thank you for the pencil," I said softly. I couldn't look at my mother. I was afraid of what might happen if I saw the same look in her eyes as I'd seen in the photograph. Afraid that I might disappear, like a piece of dandelion fluff in the wind. *Soof.*

Heidi ate two helpings of pot roast at dinner, but all I wanted was a cup of ginger tea. The dream had felt so real, I kept looking at my fingers to make sure they were all still there.

Heidi made a big fuss when my mother brought out the blueberry crumble. I said I wasn't feeling well, and asked to be excused from the table.

"Where's *she* going to sleep?" I asked my father when he checked in on me a little later.

"If by *she*, you mean *Heidi*, she was nice enough to offer to sleep on the couch until you're feeling better. It's a lucky thing it got delivered yesterday."

"Very lucky," I said.

He started to leave, then stopped.

"At some point you're going to have to tell us what you're so upset about," he said. "I understand you're worried about Duck, but I gather there's something more going on. Something about Heidi and your mother, and until you bring it out into the light, it's going to take root and grow inside you like a weed."

"Blah, blah, blah," I said, pulling the covers over my head.

He stood there for a minute waiting for something else. When I didn't give it to him, he turned out the light and closed the door.

CHAPTER FIFTEEN

More than a willow loves to weep

In the morning when I woke up, my father had already left to do some things at work, and Heidi and my mother were sitting in the backyard having tea and banana bread.

I got dressed and quietly made myself a piece of buttered toast, which I carried back to my room along with a glass of orange juice. My stomach felt fine, but I wasn't planning to tell my mother that. If I had to play sick for the whole week I would, as long as it meant I didn't have to be around Heidi.

Eventually my mother came inside to see if I was up yet. When I told her my stomach was still upset, she felt my forehead with the back of her hand.

"You don't feel warm to me, sweet—" She caught herself. "Aurora. Maybe what you need is a little fresh air. I was thinking I might give Heidi her quilt today—would you like to be there when I do that?"

"Why should I be?"

My mother sighed. She looked tired, and there were dark circles under her eyes.

"Things have been tense between us for weeks," she said. "To be honest, Aurora, I don't know how much more of it I can take. If there's something you have to say to me, won't you please say it and put me out of my misery?"

"Fine," I said. "You want to know what I think? I think you should never have had me if you didn't want me in the first place."

My mother placed one hand on her chest as if she'd been shot. I flashed on the heart-shaped charm with the arrow going through it on Lindsey Toffle's bracelet.

"What on earth has happened," she said, "to make you think that you weren't wanted, Aurora? When Heidi passed her luck along to me—"

"Stop it!" I shouted. "I never want to hear that stupid story again!"

"I don't understand," she told me.

"Blah, blah, blah," I said and covered my ears.

She left me alone for the rest of the morning. Saturday was normally my TV day, but the television was in the living room, and I didn't want to risk running into them. By noon I was so hungry I had no choice, so I snuck out to the kitchen to make myself a peanut butter and jelly sandwich. There was a note on the counter from my mother, saying that she'd gone to the grocery store, and next to it was a peanut butter and jelly sandwich on a plate, with waxed paper wrapped around it. She'd signed the note, *Back soon*. Suddenly I wasn't hungry anymore and pushed the plate away.

"There are some leftovers in the fridge," said Heidi, who'd appeared in the doorway, wearing a long flowered dress and leather sandals. Her dark hair was woven into a fishtail braid, which hung over one shoulder. I hated to admit it, but she was beautiful. "Do you want me to heat up a plate for you? Or I could make you a bowl of soup if you like," she offered.

"No thanks," I told her.

She smiled.

"Soup always makes me think of Mama. Bernie had this thing she made up when she was trying to teach Mama how to use the can opener—"

"Lift up, put the can under, listen to the hum, done," I said.

Heidi looked surprised. "How do you know about that?" she asked.

"I know all the Heidi stories," I said. "My mother is obsessed with you, in case you haven't noticed."

I held up the note she'd left for me as proof.

"*Back soon,*" Heidi said. "That's something Mama used to say."

"*I know*," I said. "You kept a list on the cupboard door of all her words. Lucky me, I know all those by heart too."

Heidi tilted her head to one side. "Is something wrong?" she asked. "I feel as though you're mad at me, Aurora."

"Wouldn't you be?" I challenged.

"If I've done something to upset you, I'm sorry. I know you're having a hard time right now. I heard about Duck."

"Did you hear that my mother accused me of setting the house on fire too?"

"I'm sure she didn't mean it," Heidi told me.

"She says a lot of things she doesn't mean. Maybe not to you, but to me she does."

Heidi looked at me. I didn't think I'd ever seen bluer eyes than hers.

"Why don't I give you some peace and quiet?" she said, pulling a baggy green sweater on over her dress. "When Ruby comes back, would you please tell her I've gone for a walk?"

"Okay," I said.

I had a feeling I knew where she was going. My mother had taken me to the cemetery once when I was old enough to start asking questions about what had happened to Heidi's mama.

"Was Heidi's mama named *Soof*?" I remembered asking when I saw the headstone with the list of names carved into the pink marble.

SOPHIA LYNNE DEMUTH
SO B IT
PRECIOUS BOUQUET
SOOF

"When a person really loves someone, sometimes they call them by a special name to let them know how they feel," my mother had told me.

"Like when you call me sweetie?" I'd asked.

"Yes," she'd said, touching my cheek. "Like that. Elliot called Heidi's mama *Soof* because he loved her."

"*Soof* means *love*," I'd said.

"Yes," she had told me. "*Soof* means *love*."

*   *   *

I was feeling a little restless, having been cooped up in the house all morning pretending to be sick. Since I had nothing better to do, I decided to follow Heidi to see if I was right about where she was going. I knew a shortcut to the cemetery, and by the time she got there, I was already hidden in the tall grass under a willow tree not far from the spot where Heidi's mama lay.

Heidi had picked some wildflowers on her way there—cornflowers and Queen Anne's lace. She bent down and set the bouquet on the ground, then bowed her head. There was a soft breeze blowing, which rippled through the clover and helped carry her words to me.

"Hello, Mama," she said. "It's me, Heidi." She paused and put one hand on her stomach. "I have so much to tell you, Mama. I'm married now to a wonderful man named Paul, and we're having a baby soon. A little girl, just like when you had me. Remember, Mama? Bernie says hello. She misses you too."

I was starting to feel a little uncomfortable about spying on her, but I couldn't leave now or she would see me and know that I had followed her. The wind shifted, and it was harder to hear what she was saying after that. Finally she stopped talking and sat down in the grass with her skirt spread out around her. She sat there for quite a while, running her fingers through the grass; then suddenly, without warning, she threw back her head and laughed. I could see that she was holding something in her hand, but I was too far away to tell what it was. She stood up and kissed her fingertips, then touched the pink stone again.

"Back soon, Mama," she said. "Soof."

I saw her tuck whatever it was she'd been holding into the pocket of her sweater. Then she turned and headed back down the hill.

I beat her home and was sitting in the kitchen eating a cold Pop-Tart when she walked back in.

"Did you have a nice walk?" I asked, nibbling the edge of the toaster pastry into a row of even little waves. Ten bites including the corners.

"Yes," she said. "But I'm a bit tired." She took off her sweater and hung it over the back of one of the kitchen chairs. "I think maybe I'll lie down for a while."

"You can rest on my bed if you want," I said quickly. "It's more comfortable than the couch, and you can close the door so it won't wake you up if the phone rings or Mom comes home and starts running the blender or something."

"That's very sweet of you to offer," she said. "Are you sure you don't mind?"

"I'm sure." I felt a twinge of guilt because I wasn't being as sweet as she thought I was. I polished off the rest of my Pop-Tart, and after checking to make sure the door of my room was closed, I hurried back to the kitchen to find out what Heidi had put in her pocket.

At first I couldn't find anything. Maybe whatever it was had fallen out. I checked again, more carefully this time, poking my fingers deep into the corners, and this time I felt something soft and damp nestled down in the bottom. I pulled it out, and dangling from my fingers was a wilted piece of clover. It was a little limp from the ride home in Heidi's pocket, so I held it in my open palm, carefully separating the leaves from each other—one, two, three I counted, and then I noticed a bit of green peeking out from behind one of the leaves. I tugged it gently, and another leaf appeared. It was a four-leaf clover! Suddenly I understood.

Heidi hadn't passed her luck along to my mother.

She'd kept it for herself.

CHAPTER SIXTEEN

More than a heart loves to beat

I could hardly wait for Heidi to wake up from her nap. I hadn't decided yet whether to come right out and tell her that I knew about the four-leaf clover, or to reel her in a bit more slowly. Finally I couldn't stand it anymore, and I went to my room and opened the door. Heidi was lying on the bed, but her eyes were open.

"Sorry to bother you," I whispered. "I need to get my sweatshirt."

"Come on in," she said. "I was about to get up anyway."

It was just an excuse I'd made up, but I went and pulled my sweatshirt out of the drawer.

"This room brings back so many memories," Heidi said. "The first night I slept in here, I told your mother the sheets smelled like sky."

"What does sky smell like?" I asked, tapping my nose once, twice, three times. My tapping had gotten worse since Heidi had arrived.

"Like this," she said, turning her face toward the pillow. "I think it's because Ruby hangs the sheets outside, instead of putting them in the dryer."

"I thought everybody did that," I said, tapping my elbows—first right and then left.

Heidi smiled.

"Not in Reno they don't. And nobody there can make a pot roast as good as your mom's either. I don't know how she makes those carrots taste the way they do. I could eat a bucket of them."

My mother would be home soon, and I didn't want to waste any more time talking about sheets and carrots.

"If you had to guess where Duck might be, what would you say?" I asked, trying not to let on how excited I was.

Heidi seemed a little surprised by the question. "Gosh. I don't know much about dogs."

"That doesn't matter. Just guess where he is."

"When Bernadette loses something, she always says, *Dear Saint Anthony, please come around, something's lost that must be found.*"

I was running out of patience; it was time to set the hook. "Look," I said, "don't be mad, but I know about the four-leaf clover. I saw you put it in your pocket."

Heidi pushed herself up on one elbow.

"You saw that?" she said.

My cheeks felt hot.

"I'm sorry," I told her. "For spying on you, I mean.

But I'm not sorry about the clover. I'm happy about that, because it means you can help me find Duck!"

"Oh," said Heidi. "I wondered why you were being so friendly all of a sudden."

"I told you I was sorry," I said, reaching around to scratch my neck. I'd forgotten to turn my sweatshirt inside out before I put it on, and the tag was making me itch. "You're still going to help me find Duck though, right?"

"I would if I could, Aurora. Truly, I would. But I'm not lucky anymore."

I ran and grabbed the piggy bank off my shelf, shaking it until a quarter fell out.

"Call it in the air," I said, tossing the coin and catching it on the back of my hand, the way my father always did when he told the story about Heidi guessing the ten flips in a row.

"I can't do that anymore," Heidi insisted.

"Yes, you can," I said. "Just try."

"Okay . . . heads."

I lifted my hand up.

"Yes!" I cried.

I tossed the quarter again.

"Tails?" Heidi guessed.

I uncovered the quarter, but it was heads again. I flipped it eight more times, but she only got it right once.

"You're trying to trick me," I said. "You could do it if you wanted to."

"No," she said, "I couldn't. I haven't been lucky for years. Not since—"

"Blah, blah, blah," I interrupted. "I know what you're going to say, but that story isn't true."

"What story?"

"The one about you passing your luck along to my mother. Tell the truth—you didn't do that, did you?"

"No," said Heidi. "I didn't."

"See! I knew it! As soon as I saw the clover I knew you hadn't given your luck away."

"No," Heidi said, "I'm not lucky anymore. I didn't give it away—it went away. That clover doesn't mean anything."

"Then why did you keep it?"

"I thought maybe it was a sign from Mama. To let me know she was watching over me and the baby. I haven't felt lucky since the day she died. I love Bernadette with all my heart, but I miss my mother. I'm sorry, Aurora. I can't help you." She stood up.

I threw myself facedown on the bed.

"I'm never going to find Duck now!" I wailed. "He's never going to come back."

The phone rang, and Heidi went to answer it. It was my mother calling to say that she'd gotten a flat tire and would be home later than she'd expected. Heidi didn't tell her I was upset.

"Everything is fine, Ruby," I heard her say. "Don't worry. And don't worry about dinner either. I can make an omelet, or we can eat leftovers. You know I never get tired of eating your pot roast, and neither does Roy."

After she hung up, she came back in my room.

"Listen," she said, "I may not be lucky anymore, but that doesn't mean I can't help you look for Duck."

"We've already looked everywhere," I said, wiping my nose on my sleeve. "And put up a million flyers too."

"Everywhere is a pretty big place," she said. "What about the park—have you looked there?"

"We don't have any parks around here," I said. "Just a playground and the community garden, and they don't allow dogs in either of those places."

"What about dog friends? Maybe he went to visit someone he knows."

"The only dog I can think of is a German shepherd who used to live near Bartlett Lake. He and Duck would sniff each other sometimes, but I haven't seen him around the last few times we've gone fishing."

"It's worth a try," said Heidi. "How far away is the lake?"

"Too far to walk."

"We could ride bikes if you have an extra one."

I looked at Heidi's swollen middle.

"Can you still ride a bike?"

"The only thing I'm not allowed to do is horseback riding, which is fine with me since I don't know how to ride a horse anyway. Come on, let's go."

*　　*　　*

I rode my bike, and Heidi rode my mother's. almost an hour to get there because we had to keep stopping so Heidi could rest.

"What are you going to call your baby?" I asked during one of our pit stops.

"Sophia," she said. "After Mama."

"That's what we thought," I said. "Is Sophia a promising name?"

Heidi smiled and scrunched up her nose.

"How do you know about that?" she asked.

"My mother remembers everything you ever said," I told her. "And so do I, even though I wasn't there."

"Paul and I both like the name Sophia, and we couldn't very well name the baby after *his* mother. Her name is Ethel."

I had tried to stay mad at Heidi, but (A) she was nicer than I'd expected, and (B) she was helping me look for Duck.

"I'm glad you're not going to name your baby Lindsey," I told her. "Because I've never known anybody with that name that I liked."

We rode a little bit farther and stopped again because Heidi was out of breath.

"Paul rides his bike all the time," Heidi panted. "His calves are as thick as tree trunks."

"Is that a good thing?" I asked.

"It's nice that he's strong," she said. "He's handy too. Bernadette always has a long list of things she wants him to fix when we come over."

"Why don't you and Paul live with Bernadette? She must be lonely living all by herself."

"Hardly." Heidi laughed. "Bernadette's got a beau."

"What's a bow?" I asked.

"A boyfriend. His name is Harrison, and he plays the saxophone in a jazz band."

"I didn't know old ladies could have boyfriends," I said.

"You better not let Bernie hear you call her an old lady!" Heidi warned. "She's got more energy than most people. She and Harrison are taking ballroom dancing lessons."

"I thought she didn't go outside."

"That changed after Mama died," Heidi explained.

"Like your luck," I said.

Heidi nodded.

"Anyway, Harrison's teaching Bernie how to play the saxophone too. That's something I don't miss. It sounds like a dying moose when she blows into it."

We passed the house where the German shepherd used to live, but the windows were all boarded up, and there was no sign of him or Duck.

"Maybe we should look down by the water," I suggested. "He likes to go in the boat with us when we go fishing."

We left our bikes by the side of the road and started down the dirt path to the lake.

"Wait," said Heidi. "Let's say it together."

She took hold of my hands, and we closed our eyes and recited, "Dear Saint Anthony, please come around, something's lost that must be found."

I guessed Saint Anthony wasn't listening though, because we called and called but Duck never came.

"We should start back soon," said Heidi. "Your mom's probably home by now, and I told her in the note that we'd be home in an hour."

"Can't we stay a little while longer?" I said. "Please?"

Heidi started walking up the path.

"I'll wait for you up there," she said. "By the bikes. But we really need to go or your mom will be worried."

I walked over to the edge of the water near the rowboat and closed my eyes.

"Dear Saint Anthony, please come around, something's lost that must be found," I whispered. "Dear Saint Anthony, please come around—"

"Aurora!" Heidi called. "Come quick!"

I was sure from the sound of her voice that she'd found something. Maybe a paw print or Duck's red collar, or maybe, just maybe . . .

"Duck!" I hollered. "Duck!" I dashed up the path and around the bend, where I almost tripped over Heidi. She was sitting on the ground with her legs sticking straight out in front of her like a doll.

"Did you find him?" I cried. "Did you find Duck?"

"It's too early," she said and there was a funny look on her face.

"What are you talking about? What's too early?"

"The baby," she said. "It's coming."

CHAPTER SEVENTEEN

More than a cradle loves to rock

I tried to convince Heidi to let me ride home to get help or at least go out on the road to try to flag someone down, but she was in a panic.

"Don't leave me," she begged. "I can't do this by myself."

I tried to get her to stand up, but she said it hurt too

much to walk. Then I noticed the front of her dress was wet and I got really scared.

"Don't worry," Heidi told me. "That's perfectly normal."

But I was still scared.

Since Heidi wasn't able to move, I tried to make her as comfortable as I could. I gathered some leaves and pine needles to make a bed and covered it with the tarp from the rowboat. Then I took off my sweatshirt and rolled it up to make a pillow for her. Heidi was sweating and moaning, and sometimes when the pains got really bad, she screamed.

"Tell me what to do," I said. "I don't know how to help you."

"Stay with me," she pleaded.

"I will," I promised.

I held her hand and didn't let go, and when she cried I cried too. The pains were getting closer and closer together, and then all of a sudden Heidi's head rolled back and she started breathing funny.

"Done, done, done Heidi shhhh," she said. "Done, done, done, Heidi shhhh."

I knew that was something Heidi's mama had said. Then Heidi started saying things that didn't make any sense at all.

"Heidi . . . Dette . . . Hello," she moaned.

"What?" I said.

"Soof . . . Shh . . . Tea."

"I'm sorry, Heidi," I told her. "I don't understand. Are you thirsty? I can get you some water from the lake, but it might not be clean."

Heidi shook her head and moaned again.

"Out . . . More . . . Back soon."

That's when I realized what she was doing. She was saying the words from the list on the cupboard door! Heidi knew them by heart, and so did I.

"Go . . . Good . . . Again," I said.

Heidi looked up at me and nodded. Her eyes looked even bluer than they had before. Like there was light shining through them.

"Blue . . . Pretty . . . Now," she said.

There were twenty-three words on the list. Heidi and I went back and forth, saying them to each other in order, and when we were finished, we'd start all over again. After a while she was too exhausted to say them anymore, so I said them for her, because I knew she needed her mama with her, now more than ever before.

The baby was coming soon, but I didn't know what I was going to do when it did. That's when I heard someone coming down the path.

"Mama!" Heidi called out.

But it wasn't Heidi's mama. It was mine.

"Aurora!" she called. "Where are you?"

"Over here, Mom!" I shouted. "Hurry!"

It's a good thing she got there when she did, because things happened pretty quickly after that. My mother called for an ambulance, but the baby clearly wasn't going to wait.

"Do you feel like you're ready to push?" my mother asked.

Heidi nodded and put her chin to her chest.

"Get behind her, sweetie," she told me. "And help her sit up a little."

I crouched behind Heidi, and she leaned against my legs. I couldn't remember where we'd left off on the list, so I started again from the beginning.

"Heidi . . . Dette . . . Hello . . . Soof . . . Shh . . . Tea . . . Out . . . More . . ."

"You're doing great," my mother said. "Both of you. Couple more pushes and we'll be there."

"Back soon . . . Go . . . Good . . . Again . . . Blue . . . Pretty . . . Now . . ."

"Deep breath," my mom said.

"Hot . . . Kiss . . . Bad . . . No . . . Uh-oh . . . Ow . . . Done."

It seemed too perfect that Heidi's baby would be born just as I reached the end of the list, but that's what happened.

"So be it," I said as that beautiful little girl slipped into my mother's waiting hands.

Done, done, done Heidi shhh.

CHAPTER EIGHTEEN

More than a moon loves to rise

Heidi and her baby rode to the hospital in the ambulance, and my mother and I followed behind. We called my father on the way, and he was outside the emergency room waiting for us when we got there.

"Why didn't you call me earlier, Rube?" he asked my mother.

"I told you already, Roy," she said. "I didn't know where they'd gone. Thank God they left the bikes where I could see them. By the time I got there, Heidi was already starting to push."

"It was so scary," I said. "I was afraid she was going to . . ."

"You should have seen our little girl, Roy," my mother said. "Aurora was so calm."

"Not inside I wasn't," I said.

My father put his arms around me and hugged me so tight I could hardly breathe.

"I'm proud of you, baby girl," he said.

"That makes two of us," my mother added.

"Blah, blah, blah," I said—and I don't know why, but we all laughed.

After they got Heidi and the baby checked in and cleaned up, we were allowed to go in and see them. Heidi was lying in the bed, and Sophia was wrapped up in a blanket, sleeping peacefully in her arms.

"How will I ever thank you?" Heidi said.

"We're so grateful you're both okay," said my mother.

"Is Sophia all right?" I asked. "I mean, you know, all right all right?"

Heidi's parents had both been mentally challenged, and even though Heidi wasn't that way, I had overheard my parents expressing some concern about the baby when they'd found out Heidi was expecting.

"Rory," my father said, putting a hand on my shoulder. "Maybe it's not the best time for questions."

"I don't mind," said Heidi. "It's the first thing I asked too, Aurora. The doctor said it's too early to know for sure, but—"

"You'll love her no matter what," my mother said.

Heidi looked down at her baby and smiled.

"No matter what," she agreed.

"How much did Sophia weigh?" I asked.

"Seven pounds even."

"Same as that bullhead I caught, right, Dad? Only Sophia is a whole lot cuter."

Everybody laughed.

We didn't stay very long, and as we were leaving, Heidi asked if she could speak to me alone for a minute.

"I want to tell you a secret," she said. "But you have to promise you won't tell anyone."

"Okay," I said.

"I used to wish that I was you."

"You did?" I asked, surprised.

Heidi nodded. "Your life seemed so perfect compared to mine."

"It could have been your life, if you'd stayed with my mom and dad," I said. "That's what they wanted you to do, you know. Especially my mom."

"That wouldn't have been fair. Your mother wanted a baby of her own, and I already had a mama, and Bernadette too. If I'd stayed with your parents, they would have had to settle for me, when it was you that they had been waiting for all along."

I let those words wash over me, wiping away my hurt, because I knew they were true.

"We could have been sisters if you'd stayed," I said.

"We still can," said Heidi. "Sophia could call you Auntie Aurora."

There was something I needed to get off my chest.

"I'm sorry I was mean to you at first," I told her. "I saw that photograph you sent my mother, and it made me mad. I saw *soof* in her eyes."

"I see the exact same thing when she looks at you, Aurora. But it doesn't make me mad; it makes me happy. Everyone deserves to have a mama who loves them more than anything in the world."

Sophia woke up and started fussing, and a nurse came in to say that visiting hours were over. I hugged Heidi goodbye, and then I kissed Sophia on the top of her head. Her hair smelled like spring.

"*Soof*," I whispered in her tiny, perfect little ear.

My parents were waiting out in the hall for me. I could tell they were curious to know what Heidi had wanted to talk to me about, but they didn't press. I wouldn't have known what to tell them anyway. I needed to think about it for a while.

My father swung by the lake to pick up the bikes, and my mother and I drove home together. When we pulled up to the house, instead of going inside, we sat in the car for a little bit.

"You were really something today," she said.

"I know—you told me that already," I said. "How did you know what to do anyway?"

"I learned a few things back in nursing school. But that was a long time ago. Mostly I followed my instincts. Besides, you and Heidi had done all the hard work by the time I got there."

We were both quiet for a while. Then my mother took her seat belt off and turned to face me.

"I've been doing a lot of thinking lately," she said.

I felt my stomach tighten.

"About what?" I asked.

"About you." She reached over and took my hand, weaving her long smooth fingers between mine. "I was forty-eight years old when you were born. There are risks involved in having a baby that late in life. I took them without thinking about what it might mean to you. That was selfish of me."

"What are you trying to say, Mom? That you think it's your fault that I'm weird?"

"You're not weird," she said.

"Yes, I am! That's why you took me to see all those doctors, isn't it? You wanted them to tell you what was wrong with me."

"It sounds so awful when you put it that way," she said. "I wanted things to be easier for you."

"Remember what you told Heidi a few minutes ago about Sophia? You said, *You'll love her no matter what.*"

"That's how I feel about you," she said. "I always have."

"I know," I told her. "So stop blaming yourself, and quit being such a worrywart. I'm okay with the way I am, so can you please be okay with it too?"

"Remember that day in Dr. Harris's office, when he said not everything has a name?" my mother asked. "You said, *I have a name. Aurora.*"

"I was pretty smart for such a little kid, huh?"

"Yes," she said. "You were."

I took off my seat belt and started to open the door, but then I stopped.

"Hey, Mom," I said. "If I ask you a question, do you promise to give me a true answer?"

"I promise," she said.

"Do you think I'm weird?"

She looked at me, and her eyes were sparkling.

"A little," she said.

For some reason we both started laughing, and once we got going we couldn't stop. Tears were rolling down our cheeks, and by the time my father pulled in behind us with the bikes we were gasping for air. He knocked on the window, and my mother lowered it.

"What's going on in there?" he asked.

"Not much," she told him. "Just a couple of alley cats enjoying each other's company."

CHAPTER NINETEEN

More than a dog loves to dig

Heidi and Sophia flew home a week later. My father drove them to the airport, and I rode along in the backseat with Sophia. She was growing so fast, the little outfit my mother had bought for her to wear home from the hospital was already getting too tight. There was a song playing on the radio, something twangy on the country-western station, and one of the lyrics stuck in my head: "I love you more than a bird loves to sing."

A few days later, my father came home from work and pulled out his phone.

"Take a look at this, Rory," he said.

He scrolled through his photos until he found what he was looking for. It was a little black puppy with a white stripe running down the middle of his face.

"There was a woman at the farmers market with a basket of pups today, and when I saw this one I asked her if she'd be willing to hold on to him until I had a chance to check with you. He's yours if you want him, baby girl."

That puppy looked like just the kind of puppy I would have wanted if I had wanted a puppy, but I didn't.

"I'm not ready," I said, and because my father was the kind of man he was, he nodded and put his phone away.

My mother's birthday came around in July, and I was excited to give her the present I'd gotten for her. It was a big glass jar filled with 1,527 jelly beans. Before Heidi had left I'd asked her if she remembered what color the six jelly beans she'd eaten had been.

"How many different colors were there?" she asked.

"Six."

"I probably ate one of each," she said.

"That's what I would have done too," I said.

I had to ask my father for an advance on my allowance to cover the cost of the jar and the ten big bags of jelly beans it took to fill it: 423 reds, 393 oranges, 276 greens, 221 yellows, 115 blacks, and 99 pinks.

My mother cried when I gave it to her, just like I'd hoped she would.

It had been hot and muggy all week. My mother said she didn't feel like going out to a fancy birthday dinner, so instead she asked my father to pick up a couple of rotisserie chickens on his way home from work.

The next morning I found the wishbones drying on the windowsill.

It had been a while since I'd dreamed about Duck, but sometimes I saw him in the clouds. I still missed him like crazy, but eventually the ache began to lessen, and day by day the hole he'd left behind grew smaller. It would never be completely gone, and I didn't want it to be. Keeping Duck's memory alive was the least that I could do after all he'd given me. A good friend is never an easy thing to lose.

Since I couldn't bury Duck, I chose one of his favorite digging spots and made a little pile of stones to mark the place where a piece of my heart would always lie. I had picked a few wildflowers, but instead of making a bouquet, I used the petals and stems to spell out the word *soof.* I felt like I should say something, but I didn't know what to say, so I closed my eyes and thought about Duck, and the words of that song came back to me.

"I love you more than a bird loves to sing," I said softly.

That didn't seem like enough, so I kept going, making up more verses as I went.

"I love you more than a dog loves to dig. I love you more than a fish loves to swim. I love you more than a bell loves to ring . . ."

The words kept coming, because when you love someone as much as I loved that dog, there aren't enough words in the world to tell them how you feel.

CHAPTER TWENTY

More than a page loves to turn

One morning in the middle of August I was lying in the back of the old pickup truck watching clouds and thinking about nothing in particular when I heard someone calling.

"Hello? Hello?"

I sat up and saw a girl standing in the driveway, straddling a bike. She had a streak of blue in her hair and a pair of cat ears pinned to the top of her head.

"Excuse me," she said, pushing up her purple glasses with a knuckle. "Do you mind if I take a drink of water from your hose? I'm totally parched."

"Are you lost?" I asked.

"No," she said. "Just thirsty."

"Do you want a glass of water instead?" I asked.

"No thanks. I'm Rosemary, by the way. Rosemary Jordan. We just moved here from California."

I climbed out of the truck and opened the spigot so Rosemary could take a drink.

"Mmmmm," she said, wiping her mouth with the back of her hand when she was finished. "Nothing tastes more like summer than hose water."

"What about lemonade?" I asked.

"Good point," she said. "Tell the truth: Do you think my legs look fat?"

I looked at her legs, which were very long and extremely skinny.

"No," I said, tapping the tip of my nose. Once, twice, three times. It seemed like an odd question to ask a complete stranger, which probably shouldn't have surprised me considering the person who'd asked it had blue hair and cat ears.

"That was totally a test," she said. "I know I have skinny legs. I just wanted to see what you'd say."

"Did I pass the test?" I asked.

"You didn't have to," she said. "I already like you because you let me drink from your hose. What's your name anyway?"

"Aurora Franklin."

She paused to think about it for a second.

"Fourteen letters," she said. "Same as me!"

I wondered how she'd figured that out so quickly.

"I'm scary good at numbers," she said, answering the question before I'd even had a chance to ask it. "And spelling too. But I totally suck at faces."

"Drawing them, you mean?" I asked.

"No, reading them," she said. "It's such a pain. I can never tell what anyone is feeling. In case you haven't figured it out, I'm on the spectrum. In California everybody is."

"Really?"

"Well, maybe not *everybody*, but lots. You know what it means, right?"

"Yeah," I said. "My mother used to think I might be like that too, but it turns out I'm just weird."

"Good," said Rosemary. "I like weird people. Did you know your shirt is on inside out?"

"Yes," I said.

"Let me guess. It's a tag thing, right?"

"Even if my mom cuts them out I can still feel them," I told her. "They itch."

"I'm cool with tags," Rosemary said, "but I hate socks. They make my feet feel like they're suffocating. What grade are you in anyway?"

"Going into sixth," I told her.

"Me too! Do you want to come over to my house this afternoon? My mother's baking chocolate chip cookies, and we've got a trampoline in the backyard. I can totally teach you how to do a seat drop."

"I can't," I said. "I'm grounded."

One day about a week after Heidi went back to Reno, I had run into Lindsey Toffle at the Dairy Queen. I was just about to sit down with my Dilly Bar when she spotted me and sauntered over to deliver a few words of wisdom.

"I'm telling you this for your own good, Aurora Franklin," she said. "My dad's an expert, and he says your dog probably got burned in the fire and went off into the woods to die. He says that's what dogs always do, and after that, the turkey vultures come. I thought I'd do you a favor and tell you that, so you don't waste any more time putting up flyers. Once those vultures are done, you're not going to want to find him anyway."

I didn't have time to think about whether it was a good idea to cuss out Lindsey Toffle until it was too late. I guess it was wrong to use that kind of language, especially in public, but it was one of the most satisfying things I've ever done in my life, even if I did get grounded for a month.

Rosemary was helping herself to another drink from the hose. I tried it too, but it tasted more like rubber than summer to me.

"By the way," said Rosemary, "do you happen to have any dog biscuits?"

I felt a pang.

"Oh," I said. "Do you have a dog?"

"No," she told me, "but I saw this skinny dog limping down the road on my way over here, and he looked like he might be kind of hungry."

I was almost afraid to ask.

"Was he black with a red collar?"

She looked surprised.

"Yeah," she said. "Do you know him?"

I didn't care if I got grounded for the rest of my life. I tore out of there like a rabbit on the run. It had to be him. It just had to be.

"Wait up!" cried Rosemary.

Even though I didn't want to, I slowed down and waited for her to catch up, because, well, that's what friends do, right?

I wonder sometimes if the stuff that happens to us—good or bad—was going to happen to us anyway, and the reason we call it luck or destiny or fate or karma is so it won't feel quite so random.

I don't know if it was luck that helped Heidi guess ten coin flips in a row correctly all those years ago. I don't know if it was luck that delivered me into the arms of the mother who had been waiting for me all her life. All I know is that when a new friend shows up on your door-step on the very same day that an old friend finally comes home, you don't waste your time trying to figure out what to call it.

Not everything has a name.

ACKNOWLEDGMENTS

I'd like to express my gratitude to the many people who supported me during the process of writing this book. First and foremost, I'm grateful to my loving and patient husband, Jim Fyfe, for the hours he spent talking to me about this story. I loved you before I wrote this book, and I love you even more now. Thanks also to my mother, Frances Weeks. Thanks to Garry Williams, David Mathis, Chief Howard Reiss, Abby Gaebel, Pam Muñoz Ryan, and Cynthia Lord, for your gentle guidance and sage advice, and to my agent extraordinaire, Holly McGhee, for her continuing faith in me. Special thanks to my brilliant editor, David Levithan, who kept his promise to be waiting for me at the end of the tunnel with lighted lantern in hand. I couldn't have done it without you guys.

Soof,

Sarah

ABOUT THE AUTHOR

Sarah Weeks is the author of numerous award-winning novels, including *So B. It*, *Honey*, *Pie*, and *Save Me a Seat*, which she wrote with her friend Gita Varadarajan. She lives in New York and teaches in the MFA program at the New School in New York City. She can be found online at www.sarahweeks.com.